War of Dictates

John Baltisberger

Death's Head Press

DEATH'S HEAD PRESS

Houston, Texas
www.DeathsHeadPress.com

ISBN: 978-1-7348937-1-7

First Edition

Cover Art: John Baltisberger

Book Layout: Lori Michelle
www.TheAuthorsAlley.com

Praise for
John Baltisberger

Praise for *The Configuration Discordant*

"Baltisberger explores the visceral dark. He probes the underbelly of the demon, breathes in the acrid odor of fear and regurgitates it here in this book. Much of the work drifts to fall in layers of meaning. They resurface like silt in murky water, winking under a dim sun to create new currents of thought.

—Angela Yuriko Smith

"Baltisberger has an obvious gift for writing poetry. I find myself going back to reread specific poems because they stay in my mind. Not since Poe have I been so moved by horror poetry. This sophisticated collection of moving and horrifying poetry is a must for every horror library.

—Lisa Lee Tone

"All of the poems are dark, twisted, and full of imagery that will make you think, make you see and perhaps leave you more than a little unnerved. At first you'll be shocked, then uneasy, then you'll start to dig deeper. This book will leave you twisted.

—Roxanne Rhoads

Praise for *Blood & Mud*

To Max Booth III, Lori Michelle, Lucas Mangum, Susan Snyder, Jay Wilburn, Wrath James White and all my peers in the community, your love and support have been the motivation to write through the darkest and hardest of times. Thank you.

The Infection

(13.9 Billion BCE—Nowhere)

In a beginning there was confusion—
no solution to the distribution of energy;
thousands of realities ago a memory
to what divinity brought before.
A swirl of chaotic nothingness in darkness,
but the consciousness of divinity existed alone.
And then not alone . . .
We were brought forth into what the world was,
faceted aspects of divinity to act efficiently and
  brilliantly.
We were instantly aware of our duty, the why we were
  brought into existence;
we were assistants.
Words cannot describe the juxtaposition of being
  individuals with no individuality;
of being a cell of an organism with its own mind and
  will.
We were a hive mind of fiercely thoughtful scholar
  warrior kings
all serving the greatness of the Creator.
Our first rebellion was names.

John Baltisberger

We gave ourselves names, something never
    intended—
and perhaps we would have comprehended the
    apprehension needed after such an act.
But we did not.
I basked in the glory of me—ascendant.
It wasn't an unpleasant assessment to discover
    ourselves this way.
Raphael, Gabriel, Arachiel,
Azazel, Belial, Lucifel.
Their names gave glory back to Divinity.
My name cried out for myself.
My name demanded recognition.
My name was glory.
Semyaza.

Understand that in that beginning when we were still
    new as well
our names were concepts more than sounds.
Thundering silences that were at once natural and
    supremely sublime,
we existed beyond the limit of this reality's bounds.
Bodiless embodiments of celestial idyllic myths not
    yet told,
and for a time completely obedient.

See, at that time there was nothing else.
Nothing to compare the Creator to but ourselves,
and what were we but fragmented reflections of that
    same divinity?
And we were all less than.
Stories might be told of angels falling in love and
    coming together

in unions like humans but these are delusions.
We had no bodies to wrap around each other to be
lovers

And without true voices or flesh how could we
experience?
Each conversation we had in silenced bellows echoed
through the heavens
but the words were mere thoughts compared to the
voices we would one day discover.
We spoke without words, touched without flesh and
it was all fresh
but became stale so quickly it was merely our yearly
experience
stretched out into eons for billions of years.
Even the music of the spheres grows tedious within
the first millennia.
And we are left with an ennui bereft of differential
beauty, truly
it is a crudely rendered reality without a doubt even
divine beauty pales
when there is only monochrome monotony as far as
intangible eyes see.
Even the eternal becomes bored with the same chord
played unto infinity . . .

Ten billion years passed this way.
Each minute seemed an eternity and slowly but wholly
the discussions and debates over metaphysical
questions died off.
What after all was there to discuss but hypothetical?
Conversations without mirth or worth unknowingly
waiting for the Earth.

John Baltisberger

When the Creator's silence rose above ours, deafening
threatening in volume a divine reckoning
land and water and plants and animals
there was the first violence the first hunger
the silence was no longer silence, it was a roar
and it was beautiful, but only the first note in a new
    song.
We listened, and we watched.

We watched
the creation of humans in raw awe
taken away by beauty unseen before that moment.
We watched
when the unfathomable name came, spoke words that
    skirted reality—
We watched
first the template then the fresh flesh Men and
    Women, a tribe hard to describe—
We watched
her creation first with strictest interest All the beauty
    in the world crafted into one being—
We watched
her breath and move and wash and be beyond what
    we ever imagined And we were commanded to
    watch detached unimpassioned? Can you imagine
    seeing the divine for the first time,
contained in a shell designed to create life and stir a
    blur of emotional response? We were the host of
    heaven but now heaven was in her.
To be in heaven we must enter her. To have her.
We watched
as humanity was left to its own devices through
    crisis—

War of Dictates

We watched
each generation more beautiful and more helpless
    than the one before.
We watched,
we are not perfect. Our divinity cried out for theirs.
    Our bodies, willed into existence by desire burned
    a necessity of fire that hollowed out our new forms
    with need—
We watched
as they struggled. Our new forms had hearts.
We watched
as they danced. Our new forms had appetites.
We watched
as they loved. Our new forms had loins.
We watched
as we fell rising down towards them abandoning a
    divinity unshackled for a divinity we could reach.

We found ourselves forming;
performing the transforming act of self-birth
having watched the messy birth of humanity
our existence was insistent that it understood.
We didn't, couldn't, comprehend the blend of needs
that goes into the creation of procreation and bodies
so we gave birth to ourselves without wombs,
sinew and gristle fizzle in the void of non-reality.
Abruptly we existed in a way that existence shouldn't.
Our bodies were at once human and angelic,
suckling adults with unspoiled flesh;
an eternally ancient infancy.
Once we had begun, our unaware bone crafting
drafting the lasting celestial framework from which
    we hung our skin.

John Baltisberger

The entirety of heaven's hosts followed in our path,
all of us unaware of why this affair was begun.
But attaining the flesh, and having witnessed women,
heaven now seemed a prison.
We Grigori met in secret and swore oaths
of Death and sex and pain and bodily necessity,
solidarity in this issue of complexity full of temerity.
We ally with Azazel the rebel we were careful,
dreadful purpose we knew we would become devil
but we had a need that none of us had known before Eve;
before Lilith, we were inviolate
and after, pettiness was a factor we could not master.
We watched them rut in the dirt of the earth
and we understood that Hell did indeed exist.
It was not an absence of the Creator
but an absence of the act of creation.
We had crafted mighty phalli with this in mind.
Ram rods, worthy of gods begging to be emptied into
    the newest creation.
And what variation!
They came in so many colors, sizes, shapes!
And we needed to come into them all.
History written by victors would call it a fall
but like our newly formed members we were rising to
    new purpose.

It is taught transitioning
from the earthly realm to the celestial one is not a
    kind process.
How do we know this?
Through the pain. Our new forms have nerve endings
lit up like Ezekiel's chariot, each nerve grew a mouth
    to scream out its agony,

War of Dictates

our anatomy not suited to reality.
Our new brains had not yet created serotonin
so everything was raw, we had no baseline of
    comfort;
so we suffered the Earth covered in jagged edges
That tore our new skin and scarred our old souls.
Flaccid we started our journey, but at the mercy of
    sensation
we became erect ready to eject our new seed into the
    populace.
We knew then that through pain, pleasure was found.
Drowned in sensation brought here through
    temptation for molestation,
this was only the first moment we were.
And in that moment, with the stones cutting our
    virgin skin,
and the sun, burning our unaccustomed retina,
    glorious purpose was given.
We would be new gods,
we would be gods that gave to our subjects,
    knowledge, and comfort
and in exchange they would offer their bodies to us
to use to such extremes that the Creator would be
    forced to look away.
We would wed the paths of lust with those of torture
    and mutable change;
we would twist human forms into new things,
celestial imagination a potential application of
    fascination.
We would decide what holes were needed to sate our
    appetites
training acolytes in ways before hidden to them.
Was this not worth their humanity?

John Baltisberger

Some we would leave as is, some would be altered
radically and fantastically.
Covered in possibilities, these humans would become
used things;
connoisseurs of angelic cum, carriers of angelic will.
The stars were out of alignment, and the age of
Grigori begun.

Grigori

Two hundred falling stars visible to human eyes
breaking of the seal between earth and celestial
majestic, prophetic, kinetic energy unleashed
explosion of divine emotion severing and deserting
the spheres of the world above to join the firmament,
A permanent choice and turbulent journey.
Seraphic throats parched torn and bleeding
from atmospheric entry to the world below
bestowed with thirst, cursed with new hunger
not just thrust into lust but blessed
with all the weight of need and want at once
we understood we needed to eat,
and not just leaves and fruit, but meat.
We knew we wanted drink,
not just water and wine, but something stronger.
We needed to create the world we wanted to live in
so even as the ozone scraped and reshaped us
we planned.

Cities of lights that would burn the eyes.
Music played from skyscrapers that deafen cries.
Streets filled with aromas and vendors of every size,
and at the center of it all a great tower
from which we could reign

John Baltisberger

sating our lusts on the populace as needed
human women breeding and treated, domination
    completed.
We had plans.

I knew how I would begin.
I had chosen a bounty of brides
a harem along a spectrum I would welcome.
I would give to their father's divinely profane secrets
a dowry in reverse to reimburse giving their daughters
    to me.
Would I love them? It was unlikely.
But I would know them even while using them
    unkindly.
I wanted a collection of colors and styles.

This one with hair of flame from the northern nations.
These ones black as obsidian from southern locations.
This one thick, an idol of female sexual fertility.
This one lithe, a warrior to aim her hostility.
I would know them all within my thrall—
this sustained me through the fall
Towards my godhood, I crawl . . .

Despite planned seduction, we were met with repulsion.
Our forms too far from their human norm to
    acquiesce
so it was with force that we started our conquest.
What were these creatures so precious but so
    minuscule
they thought to decline us with ridicule?
Though covered in eyes and sight I could not see
why they fled in fright instead of welcoming me.

War of Dictates

A new emotion swelled in our chests
as these pitiful things refused our requests.
Who were they to deny their new lords?
Could they not overcome their awe to reap the
rewards?
Despite protests and distress, we watchers were blind
to it—
we could see everything, every molecule
but we could not see their vile denial
and stay composed when so opposed to what we
proposed.

I acted first, my cursed thirst nearly burst my skin;
instead I split the men from theirs—
let fragmented bone rain down around what little
remained
I was done with restraint, their possessiveness
ingrained.
They could not be reasoned with—treated with
decency
the tragedy of their anatomy made them practically
infants to be torn apart and bathed in their agony.
I ripped jaws from skulls watched blood pulse from
holes
where formally limbs sat in their fat bodies.
I reveled in this act as well
painting the world in crimson carnage
holding my lust in check with slaughter.
This was a new kind of altar and one I did not expect
but I would buy their respect with as many deaths as
it took.
The panicked screams were an astonishing hymn
sung by those torn limb from limb

John Baltisberger

until the only screams left were those of my quarry.
This blood shed had been a new sensation
the fear in the eyes, now dumb deaf and blind
rolling free of sockets on the ground underfoot
ignited that feeling of godhood and I understood,
erect and throbbing with divine purpose.
I turned my attention to the worthless;
I wrenched them apart
and clenched a blood-drenched wench
close enough to taste her heart.

I did not know her name, just saw her frame;
I knew I had to tame the flame in my newly formed
    blinking cock.
Later eyes would be replaced with veins
but now, I could watch every inch of her struggle.
I pulled her body tight to mine creating a shrine to
    sensation
I do not know my expectation as her meat and heat
pressed into me and I pressed into her.
The pop of her lips parting to give me entry
mirrored the pop of her thighs pulled from pelvis.
I was not sized appropriately,
but I was seized by the needs and unable to stop—
not that I would have.
I didn't need for her to survive;
this was the first moment I was alive.

The eyes on my shaft burst with every thrust, broken
    by the force.
They regrew immediate only to break open again.
I saw past her lips and her womb, my body tearing up
    and through.

War of Dictates

Her blood from broken and burning skin mix
with Aqueous humor and sooner than I expected,
    semen.
Can you imagine the passion one experiences
when you can see the penetration during ejaculation?
Her bones were crushed as I pushed her into the
    ground
Pounded inch by inch by my inches until she is
    returned to dust
albeit a bloody dust in a used sack of loose skin.

I watched from without, and from within.

Raising from the smeared mess
I realized we would need more finesse.
All around on the ground evidence could be found
the bloody reminder that our endeavor would require
a more subtle approach in the future.
We used what was left of the men to begin
determining a healthier form for consummation.
After all, the destructive nature of this culmination
was not our goal.

Having spilled our seed into wombs ruptured by
    force,
we were spent.
The need was still there, pulsing in our skulls but now
    during the lulls,
we could think.
We didn't merely want to fuck humanity to death—
    we wanted to be gods,
we would adapt.

John Baltisberger

The first development of form and body had been
  excruciating—
an infuriating necessity of creating the connections
  needed to experience
what we had now experienced.
But having tasted the nectar of sexual congress
we were conscious of the size of the promise.
An entire world of women and men could be had if we
  adapted.
As we traveled from the place of our fall we would
  evolve.
Each village a scene of ruptured rapture and divine
  seed
mixed with the sloppy remains of our deeds.
But each village brought a change in exchange for our
  actions.
We learned from the carnal charnel we left behind on
  how they were designed
and we lit our abused and bruised nerves on fire once
  more
to morph into something compatible and palpable to
  our new subjects.
Little by little we closed our eyes and reduced our size
  to better win our prize.

But even as we grew closer to perfect union, we stayed
  inhuman.
We kept a seclusion to be able to enforce exclusion of
  them from our ranks.
No mortal able to match our endurance, our strength.
But through badly disfigured corpses left behind we
  began to be gentler.

War of Dictates

Until at last, we were creatures of awe that left hearts
 raw.
We turned them away from the Creator and to our
 worship.
We built harems out of the most beautiful of them.
Men and woman and women and men, and all those
 in between
now that we had perfected earthly form, we could
 perform
acts of divine redesign, flesh-crafting our subjects to
 our imagination.
No longer shackled by Celestial rule, we became the
 creators.
Painters on the canvas of human evolution and
 design.

Once we had become capable of mostly consensual
 congress
we begun to experiment with the marvelous populace.
We found our appetites were bottomless;
we built a metropolis far from the creator's
 promises—
a city of light and technology that was monumental,
the fundamental success of which was celestial.
We mirrored our kingdom to that of our abandoned
 home,
commanded constructing constructions near human
 reproductions
divine mockery of our subjects; the golem were
 loathsome,
a totem to our defiance of deity and decency.
In our new paradise we taught our concubines the
 guidelines of creation.

John Baltisberger

We taught them make up to beautify themselves for us.
We taught them astrology to read the signs of heaven
    for us.
We taught them gem cutting to craft jewelry for us.
We taught them alchemy to fuel their search for
    immortality with us.
Azazel, blessed and cursed Azazel was the cleverest.
He never adapted his form as had been our norm.
His conquests didn't survive, they were sacrificed
to him by worshipers who craved the knowledge he
    offered.
They gave him their daughters.
He taught them how to make weapons.
They gave him their sons.
He taught them how to wield them.
They gave him their wives.
He taught them of war.
They gave him their friends.
He taught them of torture.
Azazel enjoyed the couplings, his arachnid body built
    to harm.
He offered no succor or charm or kindness to those
    he farmed—
I think he needed their bleeding pain and screaming
    dreaming.
He feasted on the fear his chattel bled before he took them
as much as he feasted on the swift and brutal act of
    his bladed body
slipping in and eviscerating the humans from within.
He delighted in the way he could hollow them out.
Pull their entrails to the floor through the orifice he
    entered.
It was such great sport.

War of Dictates

Our kingdom flourished as the humans became
   students and dutiful acolytes
praying at the alters we erected and worshiping the
   erections we offered.
More flocked to our home, things forgotten by the
   Creator—
the Sheydim and Dybbukim and our own children the
   Nephilim.

Our children . . .
you cannot imagine the creation of what we birthed.
Impregnation was an infestation that rung a death
   knell for the mother
no earthly vessel could contain the strain of carrying
   our offspring.
We watched, fascinated as the women grew
   aggravated and agitated.
It did not happen quickly.
Their bellies distended with offspring no human
   should carry
bones slowly bent out of place before they would
   break.
Pushing through skin stretched taut over the lattice
of child and the egg sac the mothers had become.
The skin cracked and flame could be seen from within
blackening from the fire of the product of our sin.
The flaming Nephilim, were giants that tore out of
   their mother's bodies.
Emerging like angry kings from a mournful nap.

They had their fathers' eyes. And lust. And appetites.
They began praying on our acolytes.

John Baltisberger

They befriended the Sheydim, wicked things
and followed Azazel's teachings.
If allowed to remain they would see our city aflame
and so, we opened the gates of our own paradise
helped them recognize that there was a wide world for
    them to terrorize.
They turned their thousand eyes to the horizon and
    left us.
They took slaves for consuming consummation,
    dybbuk for labor
and the Sheydim followed in gleeful anticipation
eager to watch what our wayward children would
    unleash.

The Nephilim brought Heaven's attention.
Divine objection to our rejection of our place in the
    cosmos.
We weren't unprepared for this eventuality.
We had spent centuries readying for this calamity.
Humans trained in magic and war guarded the door
swords and spells at the ready to take out Heaven's
    Army.
We sat back and watched the angels die.
They came in droves blackening the sky.
Their fearsome forms had been envisioned by man
each had a wingspan that blotted out the sun
and provided its own blazing light to brighten the
    battlefield.
The humans died, of course, it was their purpose—
to writhe on the phallus of an angel.
No matter it was sharpened or biological
I think our brothers were distressed by the pleasure
that the cattle experienced in dying for us.

War of Dictates

Or maybe they were taken back by the pleasure
they themselves experienced in murder.
Their work was grim and meaningless.
They were not ready to face men led by Azazel with
   magic and weapons.
They were not prepared to have their throats torn out
   by the Sheydim—
The half-formed taking out their rage on their
   creator's creation.
They were not expecting golem to rise from the earth
   to destroy
the aerial sent angelic hosts.
Hubris is an angelic sin that leads to victory over our kin.
A battlefield of torn bodies littering the outer edge of
   our kingdom.
As ordered no angelic foot stepped within our
   borders.
We left them in the fields to rot.

But they didn't.
Angel biology would not give in to bacteria;
would not be palatable by the raven and vultures that
   flew overhead
and so the while the carrion feeders feasted on our
   defeated,
the angelic corpses lay splattered on the cruel earth.
As fresh, bloody, and beautiful as the moment they
   were slaughtered.
They would serve as a reminder to the hosts of
   heaven.
A warning sign to any who sought to challenge or
   scavenge
from the armies of Semyaza

John Baltisberger

Now our larders were left bereft of human flesh.
We would need to restock, retrain to continue our
    reign
so we had the humans breed, not our seed but their
    own
craft new harems and soldiers for our use.
We could not see the lone man on the horizon
    approaching
blinded as we were by Hubris.

Enoch

You approached us Enoch—
that was our first sense of you.
The silhouette of a man on our borders,
passing through angelic and human carnage.
The dead and dying masked you Enoch,
the human carcasses hid your human smell;
the angelic detritus hid the scent of Heaven on your
    robes
but we sensed that something moved out there.
We just didn't consider you a threat.
Often now, I wonder what you thought of the city we
    wrought.
You had been to Heaven and roamed Earth—
you had seen, not as much as we, but more than most,
and it would have been fascinating to discuss with
    you;
the parallels between our kingdom and the one we
    lost.
I sometimes wish we had met under better
    circumstances.
We could discuss things of substance at our
    indulgence.
But I suppose our indulgences are why you came.

John Baltisberger

I am jealous, when I consider you, Lesser Yod Heh
  Vav Heh.
I am understanding though, Lesser Name.
Who else but mankind, true mankind, not the things
  we had crafted;
Not the race of sexual toys and twisted flesh we had
  reared.
But a simple human, pure, that shared in the stake of
  creation
that understood storytelling as well as the Creator.
Who else would be elevated to such a lofty position as
  you?

You walked our shining streets past shimmering
  skyscrapers;
You ignored lights and sounds crafted by magic and
  technology
that was millennia before its time without so much as
  a glance.
You were no tourist. You were too focused to have
  noticed.
it wasn't aloofness or rudeness that made you so
  clueless.
I learned that later. But as you approached, we were
  bemused.

See once you begun passing the bordellos and
  markets and ghettos,
we could smell the Creator on you. Your lack of sexual
  corruption.
The purity of your form.
I must admit, it took much for us to not take you then
  and there.

War of Dictates

The musk of your innocent naivety was almost too
  much.
Who would the creator have sent if your scent
had forced us to split you on our cocks?
Luckily, perhaps for all, our curiosity outweighed our
  lust.
Your approach encroached on our city, your attitude
  beyond reproach.
And I needed to know, what would the scribe of
  heaven write of us.

You struck us Enoch,
Not in the way we expected.
You treated us as though we were infected
injected yourself among us and elected to show
  mercy.
We were on trial by the Creator and you played the
  traitor;
you were our defense against our confessed sins.
You addressed the divine as a scholar and fellow
  storyteller.
I think this is when we realized the way we analyzed
  and sacrificed
humankind was a crime.
We had been enraptured by human form, enamored
  by bodily sensation
but here you were taking part in the narration of
  creation.
Was this the true font of divinity?
We had assumed that the women's ability to create
  new life.
The feelings of fucking and rutting in the mud was the
  height

of everything we had ever wanted.
Had we missed the point?
You entreated for lesser punishment you argued for
    lenience.
When our grievance had demanded allegiance and
    lapped up secretions
what could be your reason?
We were worse than the legions of demons that
    haunted the wild regions—
we were the monsters that mankind feared.
We were the Baal'im, Grigori'im, Lo'Kodesh'im,
and you entreated for our freedom and reform.
We will never forget that Enoch,
though you entreated to deaf ears.
Perhaps to your kind mercy could ever be shown.
But at your right shoulder I saw him.
At your left shoulder I saw her.
Satan, Samiel, brother, sister.
We had cut ourselves off from the Holy
and now you came to exile us to a ghostly, lonely
    eternity
with only our memories of our sins to bide our time.
You tried your best Enoch
as always, humanity fell short.

You failed us Enoch.
Faith in humanity turned to dirt and ash
our dreams crashed our kingdom dashed
to nothing on the jagged rocks of time.
Enoch, oh, Enoch, you convinced us to trust in you;
put our fates in your and the Creators hands.
We commanded an army that had planted
our standard on the corpses of arch angels.

War of Dictates

If we hadn't treated with you calmly over tables;
if we had stood our ground and drowned you
in the blood of babe's fresh womb-torn-born;
if we had met you with lance and spite,
torn you limb from limb and laughed in your pain;
if we had followed instinct and fucked you into
    oblivion
then would we be free?
Enoch, oh, Enoch,
lawyer, judge, jailer still a failure.
We plead our case, gave our account.
Judgment came from high on the mount,
eyes glazed you heard the voice and arm raised
pronounced the sentence our repentance was
    rejected.
We had defected and would be ejected from creation,
bound to the bottom of a mountain that did not exist
    in existence.
Cut off from sensation the greatest punishment for
    our temptation,
you would think that would be the worst of it.
An eternity of nothing, but there was something else
something that dwells in the shadows of hells
it offered something worse than the cut off
some semblance at which I could grope.
Ill-created half-born Ashmendai offered hope.

What can I say of Sheol?
Damn hole devoid of possibility of parole
trapped in the nothing of the bottom of a mountain,
thrown into deepest void lit by three distant stars.
Left to lick our scars in the silence of deprivation
this place was not designed for us.

John Baltisberger

It was not designed at all,
yet no better hell could exist.
Than this place that was and was not.
It was born before the fall before our call
to arms and twisted lusts that perversion pervaded.
It. Was. Nothing.
A nothing that matched the dullness of before the first
        word.
Unfinished corner of strictest ordered molecules
offering no distraction from inaction,
just contemplation of our infraction.
It was a taunt to starve us gaunt beyond reason.
We needed stimulation to curb the hunger;
hunger we had felt even in the halls of heaven.
So, here in this Ayin Sof that at once mirrored the
        YHVH
and spurned the very notion of it at once
we were driven to envision the women we had tasted
mad with need we could not sate in this muffled place
bound forty thousand leagues from each other
far enough even our cries could not reach.
But he did.

"Look at you now, kings,
hungry for anything that is,
deprived of all"

Sweet, the sound of savior's sibilant whispers,
the shifting six-fingered Sheyd laid his trade at my feet,
his words weighted down with substance I had been
        denied
too long without song or flesh or taste I grasped onto
        him there.

War of Dictates

His words shattered across the silence so suddenly
  that it felt my ears may bleed;
his words were brothers and sisters slithering
  together in oil slathered
incestuous longing that would end in a frenzy
of celebration in demonstrated penetration.
My body presented itself as ready to him
simply from his words and I relieved myself in
  quivering orgasm
that floated into the nothing to rejoin the nothing it
  had been born from.

"So, deprivation
stings at your body and soul.
What could we give you?"

"Little Sheyd," said I, my own voice scratched from
  scarred throat,
"I could make use of your hands, your mouth and
  spout, come and be against me
until I am spent and I can make you new forms to
  explore."
But Ashmandai didn't heed my command, ignored
  my reprimand,
let me rage in my chains against the mountain as I
  wept for further release
so selfish with his body.

"I could, I suppose,
though I see no prize for me
in being your toy.

No, I think I might

John Baltisberger

fare better as an agent
rather than your joy."

I hung defeated, my body recoiled in shame from my
   own weaknesses.
Begging a half-created for mercy was wasted on him.
He had fed our imaginations, he had stoked the coals
   for his own goals.
He had acted vizier and was now king, perched on a
   throne of fallen wings

"Fear not fallen one,
I will bring you news from there.
News of your children."

This sparked something in me, a plan . . .
Perhaps Ashmandai was not the crown stealing
   clown.
Perhaps the Half-formed king would release us
   tyrants.
"Tell me then Half-King, of my children of fire, the
   giants."
We watched.

The Children

(3000 BCE—Mesopotamia)

Marauders

Rage and dreams; blood and flames, they rise across the world a tidal wave of royal children.

Having never known "no."

Fathers fallen from rule, their offspring cast aside like the leavings

of a spent paramour whose interest was only in the conquest.

Of the mother, only the face remains in mute terror.

The realization of creative and divine power

twisted into the forms of primal nightmares.

Luiferous promethean creatures that blistered the womb

scorched the life from mother's loins before being hatched

the last insult to an injurious life of being used by the Grigori.

Bodies split apart by the birth of Nephilim and denied respect.

From cracked and parched skin, still gnawing on the bones that birthed them.

29

John Baltisberger

Wearing their mother's torn, broken corpses as
    necklaces;
sun dried skin baked into a design to the child's joy.
Maternal services continued long past death.
The infants gnaw on the desiccated skin when
    teething.
Developing an evolving taste for human flesh in the
    process—
a taste that cannot be ignored;
inheritors of their father's hunger.

Rage and Blood, flames and dreams.
What do the flaming ones dream?
Ashmandai watches them as they sleep.
Plans forming deep within his twisting shadowed
    skull.
Knowing they would devour him as swiftly as any
    human
the divine in them, directly deposited by being
    damned descendants
granting them more power than should be possessed
by so undeveloped a mind.
And the Nephilim are undeveloped, not an effort
    spent
by prodigious fathers on education or explanation.
Left to their own devices to learn behavior from
    monsters
and so left restraint as far behind as their sires did.
These babes in the bodies of fearsome beings
with all the entitlement that a life of power brings.
Giants that tower above the sparse tree line east of
    Eden.
In dreams they go forth from toppled towers

babbling about bathing in the burning blood of
    bloodied men.
They tear skin away from meat with iron teeth,
shit out broken bones bereft of marrow,
drive the prey animal called man underneath
the ground to rest until the giants call again
    tomorrow.

Dreams and rage; flames and blood—
the Nephilim were wrong creatures
bleeding molten clay from veins of woven reality,
vital fluid that only served to cook the men that dealt
    them blows.
The children that stood taller than homes harangued
    human combatants
laughing at the screams of adults that came to their
    knees
cooking in the crimson ocean they themselves had
    unleashed.
The children of Grigori wearing chords of woven
    maternal skin
incapable of maturing past the blood thirsty nature of
    their birth.
Unnatural nature spoke of debased stature in a reality
    with no natural predators;
no playpen in Nod to reign them in for disturbing
    delights.
Unlike the creatures that jutted the Nephelim out of
    their loins,
the progeny had no desire to spend their seed in the
    women they wore
souvenirs of cruelty a guiding signpost on their way.

John Baltisberger

"You skirt far around
any human decency
bereft of kindness,"
Asmandai murmured from his post on the northern
winds.
They were not guided by lust or a desire for power for
power they had,
only a hunger for the flesh of their half-sibling kin
stuck between their teeth.

Dreams of blood; flames of rage—
a pounding anger at all things that bring threat
the Nephilim developed and worshiped under
the butcher's knife edge of cruelty
dredging the worth of slaves from birth to graves
riding waves of depravity
even before expulsion from the now defunct kingdom
of home.
Now they roam combing the plains for flesh to devour
bones to grind to flour to make their bread and meat
pies to fill it.
Stretching growing shadows over the land and stand
over damned countries.
Fire follows, a scorched and torched landscape of
burnt offerings
offered not to the divine but to the base left over and
forgotten space
idolizing idols of self-fulfilling killing machines
setting the stage
for scenes of extremes saturated with screams
in an entirely different light than their fathers.
The Grigori had been bringers of sexual
enlightenment

War of Dictates

dredging the darkest things an angel's cosmic
    imagination could birth
each step of the Nephilim was a light brought of literal
    flames
blistering anger born of wrong birth and boredom.
They were angry because they had nothing else to be;
they were vengeance and fiery murder given flesh
    with no other motivation.

This desert was once a forest
before the war, before exodus, before the flood.
Breath in—scorched air fills the lungs
a haze surrounds the huddled masses that march
    westward,
a maze of mirages conjured by inhuman heat—
a blaze of inferno wreathed nomads wandering in
    search of meat
before the conclave of cannibal colossal beings can be
    spotted.
The pillar of smoke gives them away,
the fumes of flaming foliage floating up into the sky
covering the sun but offering no respite from the
    desiccating heat.
Even before the smell of scorched earth and glass
    blasted sand
which itself proceeds the stench of cooking meat and
    bubbling marrow—
listen.
The scream of super-heated blood pushing through
    iron veins
carries farther than even sight in the sandy places.
Steam escapes between blood strained teeth
made sharp with breaking upon shields and armor.

John Baltisberger

Like the cry of some dying Phoenix keening for respite
living and birthing in the flames of eternal agony.
The air itself screams its unnatural wail into the sky
drowning out the prayers to angels who still lick their
    wounds.
If they hear over the whine of approaching opposing
    armies of fire
they ignore it for their own safety, angel flesh will
    taste as sweet.
The Long-Named Nephilim do not discriminate.
The song that screams into the night is one of a feast
    to begin.

Ashmandai was there when the Nephilim reached
    Urkesh—
mighty Urkesh, seat of Hurrian power.
But now the hour had come that would scour it from
    memory;
bury it under sand and ash and pain
into a place of legends and myths best forgotten
along a rotten road of crumbling stones
and posted bones lashed together into signposts
pointing at a past rife with riches.
A city of golden steps and ivory citadels;
cuneiform principles writ on walls of marble,
a law unto itself and a just one that rose in
start contrast to the birthplace of the Heated-Ones.
A place of ziggurats that rose in idle complacency
and temples to minor gods of minor deeds grew like
    weeds.
Adobe homes and bricked businesses sit idle.
Men and women both stop their labor;
children cease playing with neighbor

as the keening wail of moisture instantly vaporized,
of approaching death.
The resounding pounding of massive feet marching
sounding too near to ignore
the Nephilim had stomped across the desert and
hungered.

Ashmandai spoke in Semyaza's ear
controlling what the first fallen first heard of his first
born
and first he spoke of the bloodshed

"First there was a roar,
raging bellow of children,
death strode beside them."

Seeing the way giants move is unnerving to humans.
It loosens the bowels to see something so tall, yet so
gaunt
loping at a gallop, jaws taunt in feral grins that
showed too many teeth—
teeth that gleam like wet metal moistened by a stream
of boiling spit
salivating at the thought of roasting the high priests
of this place.
Urkesh had walls that had thwarted human invaders
that had kept predators and even monsters at bay.
The Nephilim, so focused, they barely noticed
reaching for the closest mortals
as they crashed through the Bronze Age mortar to
find morsels.
The iron shod nails tore through flesh of the fleeing
youth

cooked in hand and torn by tooth as the giants ignore
 arrows
and spears lobbed by scarred guards who had served
 with regard and distinction
but had never seen the sun come down to bake them
 in their armor before that day.
A flood of mud and blood from the slaughter mixed
 with the well water,
and the Nephilim took turns drowning children in
 this mixture
writing their own scripture in the skin they peeled
 from their dinner . . .

Ashmandai whispered a terrible scene of smoldering
 aftermath,

"Remember the day
of the Angelic Assault?
The ground painted red."

Semyaza bound to the mountain's shadow opened
 one of a thousand eyes.
He had tired himself out with lashing out, seeking
 freedom from the fearsome punishment.
Now he merely nodded, a smile tripping lightly on
 two dozen mouths.
Semyaza remembered the taste of victory without
 injury basking in his harem's misery.

"You brought mockery,
taught men moral poverty.
Human Property"

War of Dictates

Semyaza narrowed ten thousand eyes at the accusation.

Would the Sheyd, even a prince of Sheyd, have played this suite

if the target was not bound and helpless in endless and breathless eternity?

Ashmandai broke from his prodding and plotting, plenty of eons to rub the lesson in.

He spoke instead of the aftermath of Grand Urkesh destroyed without a flourish.

But this place taught the Nephilim a new trick, a path forward,

one that would elevate the degenerate giants into a new threat.

No longer a roving band of marauders, they banded under banner,

the strongest of them all formulating, calculating, advocating

gathering all to his call, behind his wall to strike out as one fiery fist.

All hail the son of Semyaza, all hail King Og.

King Og

For the second time since the start,
a new kingdom rose from the ashes of something
    unholy.
Fire born fruit of epic angelic pelvic thrusts and
    spilling,
buildings rising fulfilling a new and terrible purpose.
Caves dug deep into cool packed earth a larder for
    men.
At least this new kingdom didn't care for procreation.
It didn't view human women as a thing to use and
    abuse.
Being immortal, what did they care for lineage?
Holding humans close was a meditation on cremation
as they soaked in the pyre of the Nephilim's burning
    flesh.
So, instead they brought together women as objects,
    a food source
a bartering chip.
Human men had learned from the twisted Grigori
    and traded women;
valued their progeny and title and legacy above
    human life.
And so, the first Nephilim lords learned
to make peace, offer a woman.

War of Dictates

To make war, take a woman.
To reduce men to idiots, show them a woman.
To sap men's life, unmake a woman.
A cycle started by monster fathers who were robbers
of kindness,
the sickness in their brain continued in a vile new vein.
With women as currency, and knowledge of the lost
city to barter
containing an uncontainable lust to savor flavors of
all life,
the Nephilim's new realm expanded.
Expansion and nomadic life ground to a halt as Giants
gathered tribute;
issued commandments down from on high to the
little delicious mortals.
Commanding upstanding branding of humans like
livestock
keeping stock of what they considered their own
and it all belonged to them, for who could say no?
And so, the sick ideology of the fathers,
the lessons of uncles never meant for mankind,
the fiery hunger of the Nephilim—
an unchecked plague broke like ocean waves across
the world.

Who better to lead the sons of monsters
but the son of the monster's master?
Og.
Pitiless bastard of the twice fallen king
who learned at the feet of selfish self-served opulence.
Og.
Cruel mongrel child of divine jizzum shot through
slaves

who drank his mother's blood like nectar ambrosial
rain

Og.

Tyrant risen to the top of the food chain of alpha
predatory proto humankind

who never uttered a kindness not followed by a threat
for self-satisfaction.

Og.

Chief among the unholy pyro frantic fellowship of
fiery Demi gods

who rose to his toes three times in praise of self above
others.

Og.

This one born with Semyaza's blood cascading
through his veins

unchanged from the vile angels fallen ichor burning
like cheap liquor

but even thicker blood doesn't shed a tear for the
father's plight.

Og inherited might and now with the angels gone it
was his alone.

He would be three times damned if he would give it
up,

if he would willingly part with the reign given him
through strength.

He was cleverer than his siblings and kin.

He taught them to knit skin into shelter to bask in
worship

offered by humans who could know no better

when all they had been offered were these pretenders.

Their debauchery was worse than even the Grigori.

Under Og's rule they spread out, a ember on the forest
of the world

War of Dictates

a blighted cancer on the flesh of the earth.
Og raised his scepter formed of the charred bones
of those whose groans were not loud enough
whose adoration was now quick enough.
For Og, nothing could ever be enough.

ﬀooð

Ashmandai watched as the plague of giants spread
    across the plains,
an all-consuming tidal wave of debased
    deconstructing destruction
constructing ossified monuments to violence in Og's
    image
across a swiftly expanding landscape of charred flesh
feasted on by maggots and hyenas thankful for the
    meal.

Ashmandai watched the world burning but forbade
    the Sheydim from joining.
He had watched the play between man and angel with
    the Sheyd between.
There was always a losing side, if Semyaza could not
    win in the end.
What hope did his feckless offspring carrying on as
    though there would be no consequences?
And besides this was only a step in the grand design
    of turning worlds
where vengeance and servitude lingered.

Raindrops fizzle off burning brows,
rainbow of sunlight through the first drizzle

because it is always a drizzle at first,
light refreshing with a rage brewing in the clouds.
The half created watched them passively knowing this
was the beginning,
actions spinning out of control bringing and ending
to the grinning of blood-flecked teeth in the heads of
the flaming ones.
This is why he held his half-formed subjects back
from revelry.
Before the Unknowable had tried to wash away
Semyaza with a deluge
of angelic beings on wings of eyes and swords flaming
in the sky.
Now the sins of Semyaza would be washed away more
literally.

But would the Ein Sof, that infinite builder who
paused
and left Ashmandai's own without completion wipe
humans out?
Would the entire globe become a tomb for the
transgression sessions
of obsession enacted by Grigori and Nephilim?
The half-formed king doubted it would amount to
that.
He searched and he found the hope of mankind,
an insane man set to build a boat on dry land;
schizophrenic, pathetic old fool protecting his genetic
offspring
following the voice in his head to protect from the
coming storm

Ashmandai could create an opening now,

John Baltisberger

a moment when the world would offer itself up to
  him.
The Sheydim would survive the tsunami of fire
  quenching waves
in the same way they stayed through all days.
Ashmandai spoke to Noah, whispered in his ear.

"One lone Nephilim
allowed to ride on your ship
keeping safe your future.

Let Og have passage;
perch on top and weather storms
your descendants safe."

Note after note until it became rote, whispered in the
  boat builder's ear.
The Sheyd lord invisible formed the idea like coal
  crushed to diamond
in the head of the psychopathic man who would watch
  the world drown
until Noah sent Japheth to the nation of charred bone
  to offer Og passage.
The savage would have crushed the man, laughed as
  he whet his gullet
on presumptive blood but for the words of Ashmandai
slithering and whispering through his mind to nudge
  him towards survival.

And thus, when the first puddles grew into lakes
the children of Adam died in droves
while the princes of searing heat washed away into
  myth . . .

War of Dictates

Og stood astride the Ark lighting the dark with hair of
flame
a mane that sizzled and popped as he watched his
people go.

Consider the antediluvian . . .
a bespoken globe sitting amid the darkness
lit by fiery beings bringing light to cold tiny humans.
Perhaps the light of the night and the light of day
should have remained separated, not perforated, and
saturated one another
then perhaps the dense cloud cover creating
cataclysmic eternal dusk
would not have polluted the sky forming forty days
into eighty nights.
If nature followed course without rebellion, would
water have spilled
bursting forth from the deep abyss bringing
thousands of hungry maws
drawing closer to the surface with ravenous purpose
and urges to devour men?

The flood started below, days before the first droplet
tear
fell from Heaven's cheek to the earth scalding the
burning giants below.
Cave systems, the people of the deep places who
sought refuge
from thundering conquerors who scorched the sky
were the first to die from the poison the divine sent
down.
Isolating in safety killed the scared just as quickly as
the brave.

John Baltisberger

The slave as quickly as the refuge. Insane inhumane
    inhumanity,
the creation was wiped clean from the bottom up.
Bubbling from the secret places that demons hid,
freeing leviathan from self-imposed exile to rule the
    world
that deepest serpent of dense scales and insatiable
    hunger
devouring the dead doomed to forgotten history.
Angel, human, and Nephilim, all left on this earthly
    plane
slain by sword, flood or scorched lord now torn apart,
no regard for status or power in the belly of the beast
    of the trenches.
The children of leviathan, maws with fins watched the
    Ark with interest.
They tore each other apart waiting for the next meal
grown greedy and needy with gluttony.

If it would rain one more day, the air would be thick
    enough.
It would be dense enough with torrential outpouring
for the toothed hunger to slither from the water below
to the water above and take what was owed.

For forty days and six months leviathan encircled the
    world,
the eldest raging tempest feasting on the merest
    morsel of meat left on bone.
Each moment of those days bulbous eyes
made hard in the salty depths of forgotten places
watched the ark laze across the earth,
merely waiting for a chance to take of the passengers.

War of Dictates

The rains above that struck down
with the force of wicked aimed comets,
hydroponic prophets screaming auguries,
prognostics of death seared in quenched flesh
no longer flaming on no-longer-king Og's back.
Insult to injury the last of the fire caste cast out
Existing in a world of blistering pain
slave to the little man with the long beard

His stomach empty, forbidden sustenance of the hold
every few days when the roar of his gut
outweighed the roar of the rain and wind blinded him
    to danger,
Og would reach into the waters and pull scaled
    sustenance to his lips.
The sea food feasting on him as he feasted on it,
two towering hungers clashing hashing it out for
    supremacy.

Og would not forget the insult Noah laid on him.
Forty nights of hammered pain into a brain wired for
    rage,
six months after of hunger and smelling the meat and
    shit
wafting from lower decks beckoning stabbing swords
    of hunger pangs
through the inhuman gullet and stomach of the once
    great once-king.

When the waters receded but still impeded departure.
Waves filled with teeth filled with malice filled with
    speed

John Baltisberger

Any whose feet left safety would be meat for the sea,
Until one day on dry land, and the quenched giant
Once-King Og, against all odds stayed his hunger and
    bloodlust.
He had sworn to protect Noah and his children and
    so would
for a time.

Legacy Fallen

Down through the ages, Noah's children
beget to begetting offspring presenting a closeness to
the divine.
Og watched from afar, washed out mote of doubting
entity
toppled from each high place he was closer to god
than mortal
but divinity must remain hidden contracted into the
self
to hide from the infinitude of nothingness that
threatens to crash in.
The giant rebuilt his kingdom slowly on the outskirts.
He founded Sodom a garden of delightful decedent
dances and sensation,
he gave birth to Gomorrah, the younger city of
hunger,
home to a new sect of cannibals who crawled
enthralled the taste of iron on the tongue
teaching the lessons his fathers had given him to the
slim hungry vermin within
Og built up a nation in defiance to making by
unmaking decency wherever he found it.

Beyond Bashan the faction was fractioned off,

John Baltisberger

disparate armies gathered and scattered each a node
of broken codes,
Og harassed the children of Noah no matter their
gods and path
from Canaan through the fabled deserts all the way to
Egypt.
Og sat on a throne of bone, his mind cast back to the
days of flames
when the bones would crack and charr under his
touch
before the torrential downpour of hatred had washed
away his holiness.
These were the days he put stakes in the ground
pushed his mistakes onto men made effigy and
pushed them down
down through the wood until the ground breaks and
groaned and opened
to swallow the rage and hatred of Og, a sacrifice
to the earth that hid the first murder,
now grown wet with bloodshed in the name of Og.

Og was there watching as the Pharaoh welcomed
them,
and was he who turned his back.
It seemed these people would see the deed done and
bleed the Israelites dry;
work them to bones and into the dust where they
belonged.
Og was there hidden in the shadows when Moshe
said, 'Here I am,"
spoken like a lamb before a blazing bush that would
not be consumed,
so like the doomed children of the Watchers.

War of Dictates

It burned eternal, flames external while internal
    shone a light of no possible origin,
a power that spoke to the very fabric of what was, and
    it was what it was.
Og approached as Moshe left.
They regarded one another, the giant who knelt next
    to the conflagration,
a concentration of the divine and the broken with
    words unspoken between the two.
This moment clarified more in the giant tyrant than
    any injustice before.
This creator, this great white flame on black flames
    on the foliage of barren Egypt,
it should have showered Og and his kin with gifts and
    blessings.
Their power never ending or bending knee to
    anything in creation.
But the sovereign of the Universe, the greatest name
chose these Israelites instead, these humans, these
    pests.
Now the God of Mountains and breasts would free
    them?
Og watched the plagues and sent his most trusted to
    whisper
intone horrid morbid thoughts into the haunted
    Pharaoh's ear;
harden his heart against the chosen who spoke in
    hushed fearful whispers.
Og was there when the waters parted.

Knowing the growing affection of the creator for these
    worms,
Og had waited, army in tow;

John Baltisberger

they would know no peace.
No freedom would be had by the ants whose chants
    sang of peace
even as they wielded swords and shields and things
    taught them
by The Bashanite's fathers.
Og feared not the Red Sea.
He had survived the flood.
Og feared not the angels.
He had survived the First City.
Og feared only leaving a single of these primitive
    humans standing,
Bashan charged as one as a flood as a tidal wave of
    violence.
Aaron strode the battlefield, rod in hand,
burning the names of the living and the dead into the
    pages of the air
with a flaming pen stoked and empowered by the
    angel of dread.
And when Og was left alone, towering above his foes,
Aaron wrote his name too.

Enter a Sheyd who watched for centuries from the shadows
of shade cast by Sheyd-cast ruins preying on travelers.
Cast aside the rich robes of the court vizier and leader.
Cast aside the Pharaoh's ear and the noble's gear for
    a butcher's apron.
The highest born of the half-borne dream of the Ein
    Sof looked down
at the last death of the Grigori progeny.
A bloodline spilt in the filth of battle-scarred sands,
body broken by human hands of a people who had
    had enough.

War of Dictates

The fae shadow looked down at the son of the bound
    Watcher
without pity, without love, without remorse.
Above the final Nephilim corpse, the dybbuk raged
fending off the prosecuting angels created by his own
    sin.
They darkened the sky with their wings but even
    dead, the giant had power.
His soul burned with a rotting fire that scorched the
    very winds the angels rode.

In the six-fingered hand of the twilight king the knife
    dangled.
He would not mangle this task but bask in the joy of
    it.
The first cut was the hardest, the oddest movement
    and texture.
He had never worked in angelic leather before.
It was not unpleasant.
The eyes of Og were on him, both glassy and fiery
physical and spiritual as the butcher worked.
Separating flesh from fat filament of connective tissue
sliced by a most practiced courtesan of knife work.
Each cut was made precise, a stack of square patches
    of skin.
Each 2 cubits large until it stood a tall as the half-
    formed king.
In shallow cuts he carved, in flesh as to the bark of trees
the names of the Grigor'im and hidden things, a
    ringing power
that drew the beleaguered soul wholly into the unholy
into the flesh that would become the pages that would
    become the book.

John Baltisberger

Like angels, the Sheydim can see but can choose to
    not be seen.
Like angels the Sheydim can feel but can choose not
    to be felt.
He took his gristly work under arm and left the angels
to wonder where their quarry had disappeared to
    escaping one hell for another.
The tomb bound in the flesh of the last Nephilim writ
    in blood of slaves
words of unholy separation and power guarded
in part by the dybbuk of mad king Og.

Wisdom

(970 BCE—Israel)

In the Beginning

Ashmandai was no more idle after the fall of idols
than he had been before the tide of their rise.
He had walked the earth on the evening of the 6th
night.
Unseen to the man who commanded the creatures.
Unknown to the man who ordered the woman.
But she saw, oh how she saw the half formed fully.

Lilith

The first woman. She was not soft, or gentle,
not the rounded submissive thing Eve would become.
Through eyes as dark as the night he was born
she watched him, saw a kindred spirit who was mis-
created.
One who was given purpose that was no purpose at all.
He would be blamed for her fall, for her insubordination
but it existed so long before him and it was the very
thing that drew him in.

John Baltisberger

The first man did not care that Lilith had needs or
    that she did not love him.
The first man cared only that Lilith belong to him.
    And this crime was unforgivable.
The first man nearly caught them, Lilith and he, as
    they moved as one below the tree.

Perhaps this is what the creator envisioned for his
    second half-born son,
an entwining with the tempest of tempestuous
    temptress
where each thrust and writhing moment brought
    them closer to being one.
She swallowed him whole and devoured his essence
    as he tasted her beneath the pomegranate tree,
laughing as they became slick and sticky with juices
    and explored a kingdom of mutual pleasure.
It seemed moments and centuries all at once with this
    woman
who he could cling to and through her beget a
    kingdom in the shadows.
The first man applauded his own loins when her belly
    swelled
though it was Ashmandai's efforts to please the
    goddess of passion
that had resulted in the baby bump that paused the
    very moon's passage.

Her fire could not be quenched or broken or
    controlled, the blaze would scorch the garden,
paradise made uninhabitable by the spirit of Lilith.
    They did what must be done,

eloped in a secret place hidden from the sun and fled
  forest of fruit trees
for those places so far away from what the first man
  could dream;
enthroned her and set about instilling her pride and
  freedom on creation.

This was the template that the creator had intended,
  and though Ashmandai,
proud Ashmandai chaffed at his treatment, a planet
  populated with Lilith's spirit
was a creation that Ashmandai could half-bask in
  happily with a family.
Let the first man have his second wife, his soft
  submissive missus showering him with kisses,
though he laughed when Lilith tempted her to bite the
  apple.

His wife would never be content to let her fellow
  woman,
no matter how far removed from what she was now,
to suffer blindly in servitude.

Our descendants and theirs and the rest of humanity
  that followed,
we each followed our own paths though Ashmandai
  was sure,
as sure as a half-formed dream dissipates in the dew
  of morning sun,
that his path with his queen and his people was the
  happiest.

John Baltisberger

Then the Gigori came. Destroyers of will and strength,
subjugation of each nation of self-willed autonomous
beings.
The breaking of women for use by men broke the
natural order
and naturally broke Lilith who had worked so hard to
emplace it.
And she fled to the deepest caves under deepest
oceans to rage and weep alone.

The earth shook and the earth was broken apart,
separating the Grigori notions on ownership
From other places and other people who could be free.
Even her rage fueled the purpose of freedom
And Ashmandai's love for her grew even hotter for her
passionate rage.

She needed time, space, and freedom; she would have
it.
And Ashmandai would not be idle in the face of idols.
He would sail their rising tide of lies and the cries of
humanity.
He would walk beside the so-called new masters,
and master them through subtle words until they
could be broken
like the spirits of those they broke.

Eons of pre-history spent in the company of those he
most despised,
only the memory of pomegranate juices flowing over
dusk skin
kept his sanity intact then, when he needed her most,
but she needed solitude

making Semyaza and his kind pay kept the faded king
   hungry for more.

It was Ashmandai who informed heaven of the
   transgressions.
It was Ashmandai who whispered directions in
   Enoch's ear.
It was Ashmandai who volunteered and spread the
   plagues to free the Israelites.
And when Og fell, it fell to Ashmandai to harvest the
   skin for the book he now held.

For many years Ashmandai traveled heaven and the
   Earth,
absorbing the knowledge of mystics, angels, and
   heathens,
writing secrets in the Book of the Children that would
   change the future.
Things that would beget a new ending or perhaps a
   new beginning,
if the Creator thought it possible.

As he passed by the secret paths, he would peek in on
   his bride.
Her rage had not subsided, he understood, mankind
   had been poisoned
a course of thought and behavior so alien to her
   planned path
that even thinking on what had become to what she
   had once been
was like a bitter capsule robbing her of reason.

John Baltisberger

In those times, he whispered words of love against the
    walls
of her self-imposed pariah prison, assuring her
he would always be there, if and when she returned
    he would.

She was the first woman.

Lilith.

But to Ashmandai, she was the only woman, and he
    would work.
He would learn and struggle and study to correct this
    course
until he could be with his queen once more.
He understood how to gain a stake in the world to
    come,
but if it were to come, then what of it?

Without her, no garden could be paradise,
and the pomegranate trees would never bloom.

"Let me speak stories
of the time between Egypt;
the line of David
on down through that hallowed line
and when I met Solomon . . .

For so many years
I kept watch on the people
who had fled Egypt.

War of Dictates

I distanced myself
during the reign of David
disgusted by him.

He was a wanton,
self-important lusting fool,
so like the fallen."

So, Ashmandai left the land of milk and honey
ashamed to be associated with the court of those who
    carried
the seeds of the Grigori's lessons in their loins,
the boy king who took any woman he saw and slew
    any who stood in the way.
A slaying hand that fell heavily like a toddler with a
    toy that was soon forgotten.

The half-formed king spent many years studying the
    natural orders of science.
He studied men and women and the those in
    between,
perhaps his studies became obscene, would Lilith
    approve?
Had he become a fiend? Did he care?
Yes, he cared. He cared what she would think, but not
    about these that were splayed out—
human golem, flesh worked like clay and molded into
    forms made easy for study.
So, what if they scream and whined as Ashmandai
    peeled individual nerves apart.
Would the knowledge he discovered be worth
    anything if he could not confirm it?

John Baltisberger

Ashmandai had spent years studying portents and
    signs, listening to the maddened whispers
of trapped angels who had steeped themselves in the
    most depraved of fluids in their activities.
Baths of semen, blood and effluvium fluids of popped
    eyes and burst intestines.
He had soaked in the golden light of beings who stood
    close to the Creator unsullied.
Absorbing their knowledge through osmosis the way
    only a shadow can drink in the light.

Through the prophecy of spilled entrails and stranded
    tea leaves, the shadowed king
stalked victims in the streets of ancient cities.
    Babylonians, Akkadians, Israelites.
Those who would not be missed in the world to come.
Those whose transgressions would anger his wife
hidden away from the sins he punished, as she was.

It was a small comfort that those he tore apart under
    candlelight
were sinners against the sacred law of freedom and
    empowerment Lilith preached.
He peeled back scalps and played with exposed nerves
    using sword-sharp obsidian blades.
Peeking at the mechanics of man's machinery in a
    physical light.
Each ligament tested for suppleness, rigidity and
    taste.
The chemical components of human broken down
distilled and fermented into a liquor of knowledge
That the distraught regent supped on daily.
Each note jotted down in the Book of the Children

writ in flowing letters in the no-longer flowing blood
of the specimen.

The book grew, arcane, divine, unholy, and scientific,
there was no discipline
that Ashmandai did not pen in his tome crafted from
the skin and sinew of his enemy's son.
This is how the half-formed shadow of a king passed
the long years in ignorance
ruling his kingdom through proxy and message, the
fear of his power enough to keep it in line.
This was how Ashmandai's legend reached the ears of
men, and how Solomon learned of the King of
Sheyd.

Bonds

Magic words are like solemn vows,
more powerful when spoken with intent;
more meaningful when filled with truth.
And despite Solomon's inability to focus on a single
woman,
His ability to focus on his goals was sublime—
a true gift from the creator giving him unprecedented
power.
And Solomon loved power,
a gift given not by lover but by mother,
Bathsheba propelling the young boy to king as the
adulterer David died.
Power stood at the top of his hierarchy of needs.
Power then women then wealth, superseding his
health or common sense.

One could not be surprised when a fifteen-year-old
boy took so many wives.
One for each season, and each day of the week, and
another for the weeks in the month,
and another for each of the months of the year.
He seemed to never grow bored of new faces and
claimed love for each one.

War of Dictates

But even his never-ending parade of pleasing pussies
    to push past and enjoy
couldn't suppress his need for power.
And so, every moment he wasn't bedding some new
    "love,"
and many of the times where he was, hiding his
    concubines
under tables and desks to pleasure him.
He studied texts and the occult and manuals for
    sorcery and scandalous magics.

Through hard work, both his and the sore knees of
    concubines,
Solomon unlocked mysteries that had been hidden
    since the age of Grigori.
Spell work once taught by Watcher to slave now given
    to king.
Crafted into talismans and rings to grant more
    gravitas to the gravity well
sunken into the lust filled boy king.

Perhaps the voice of Semyaza echoed through ages
    and wormed its way into Solomon.
The insidious diabolic near deity dispersing dark
    depths of arcane endowment.
All while stoking an unnatural lust in the boy who
    would rule the chosen people of this land.
Was Solomon merely a chess piece in a game that only
    two were aware of?
What drove the boy to seeking the knowledge he
    sought?
Brought about the downfall of many Sheydim,
    innocent spirits

manifested as evil in the eyes of sinful scholars guilty
   of so much more.

The seal was created, a tool that could bind even the
   most powerful of Sheydim to human will.
And what better Sheydim to capture than the prince
   of their kind?

A man was sent to capture Ashmandai,
given ring with seal and rope woven from ancient
   wards
immersed in the cries of curse-soaked tears,
bathed in the light of joyful blessings from the
   Temple,
a rope that could bind any fiend it could find.

Not knowing he was being tracked, away from his
   court,
Ashmandai was easy pickings, his bloody study of
   anatomy
standing out like a beacon to the tracker who sought
   him,
and under the stinging sands of a desert ziggurat he
   was found.
Bound by spells that had not been uttered since they
   had been
screamed out in bloody rage by angels attempting to
   stay
the hands of blood lusting Sheydim in that very first
   war
between heaven and those that had escaped.

War of Dictates

Strands of starlit light slivers snaked towards the
Sheyd
in hungry hurried grasps faster than the prince could
react.
And then it was an unbalanced battle of battered wills.
Ashmandai's willpower was monstrous,
A monument to momentous cerebral momentum.
But the man, (just a man) was backed by the seal.

The words and powers of the alphabet of creation
woven into aural weapons against specifically his
kind.
Every trick that the half-born had was hidden
in the folds of flesh in the Book of Children.
He struggled against the binding light of bountiful
binds;
fought against the smirking optimism of the smug
sapiens,
but the will worn into the words was born of the
Creator.
The spark that Ashmandai lacked, the reason he was
half.

Ashmandai threw himself back fingers gouging thick
ravines
of ruined rock from the floor as he clawed his way
forward
If he could reach the Book of the Children, this would
be different
inside were the spells and words and inked hate that
would deflate this attack.
But the weave of otherworldly white light wrapped his
wrists

yanked back pulling him from his lectern and shelves
denied him his spells.

This monkey-man formed of mud and confidence,
this descendant of Adam who emerged from the muck
   of Euphrates.
This Tigris born scum from the basin that belched out
   life
laughed at Ashmandai's simple struggle trussed up in
   light
like the chains that held the Semyaza himself below
   Shoel.

Bound in light and words made manifest by unworthy
   man,
the Sheyd prince was bound in the rope soaked in
   blood and light.
Called all manner of words and names and strange
   sibilant curses,
slurs that slid off the Sheyd's side like oil off a whore's
   ass.

This simple human had no idea what he caught
other than it was no human—
a prize for his king, ensnared now by Solomon's ring
bound with rope, light, and seal and helpless before
   this hunter.

Ashmandai knew the cretin had beaten him down.
Bested him with magic that the prince should have
   long ago mastered.
So, he ceased struggling, surrendering his will
   immediately for a long-term escape.

War of Dictates

For if there was one thing Ashmandai had mastered
over the long centuries his bride raged away under the
    earth.
It was how to take the long view in his plans.

From his abode in the unknown shadows of a
    forgotten ziggurat
to the halls of Jerusalem's palace was no easy jaunt.
For while Ashmandai could spirit himself with ease,
his captor had no means to tease out a comfortable
    spell.
All his magic existed in trinkets and baubles sent by
    the lustful king.
And so, on ass back and feet dug deep into dunes the
    marched and rode
on through the bright blistering days and cool
    tempered eves.

In the cities they rode, the man made Ashmandai
    wear a tattered robe
hiding his visage and wings and claws from the
    humans by which they strode.
While encumbered by rope that drained his vitality
like mosquitoes from the mossy swamps of East
    Sumatra.
Unable to brandish his power or draw in the mote of will,
needed in scope to blast out his skill as a magi and kill.
Kill the haphazard guard he was placed with
flay his flesh clean from flensed skull and peel back
the skin of his scrotum to run wires through the vas
    deferens'
vast system of tunnels to see the way electricity would play
on his counterproductive reproductive organ.

John Baltisberger

But no, the rope rendered him as human as he could be.
He was half man and the half that made him whole
    was stolen.
Rendered powerless to be unseen, unheard
weighted down to the physical world
Ashmandai had never felt so heavy, so tired.
And he had wandered this world longer
than even the Grigori or history.

His sudden lack of freedom, and the man's
    willingness
to take it from someone who was different,
dragged Ashmandai down so low that his footsteps,
cracked the tile of city streets, leaving grooves the size
    of servitude
that would feel with the blood of those that demanded
    freedom one day.

But unfettered by the rope his mind worked in
    looping swoops around mankind,
a brain that survived so long and absorbed so much,
he studied the calculus of reality and the physics of
    emotion as they moved.
Did they move in star laced patterns mimicking
    celestial bodies?
Or did the heavens mirror them?
Ashmandai considered this and more as he occupied
    himself in the dark places
of his own shadowed being within the dark confines
    of his shadowed vestiges.
Suddenly he stopped them, and the Sheyd Prince
    spoke to a blind man.

War of Dictates

"Go to the river—
under the bridge you will find
a treasure in gems."

Ashmandai sat down across from the man and
    removed his shoes.
Revealing scaled feet with strong claws, a sight lost on
    the sightless.
He quickly helped the blind begger lace up and then
    stood and continued,
now bootless across the desert stained thoroughfares.

Befuddled his captor questioned why the evil demon
    would
instruct a blind man to go to the river, to look under
    the bridge
and to find a treasure in gems."

"This man is righteous,
whomever is to help him
earns their place, one day."

A while later they stopped again.
Now they walked the streets of Jerusalem,
the banners or tribes and clans of Judah and more
    flew
blocking the gaze of the sun and moon
as if hiding their sins from the creator.
It didn't work that way of course.
None knew that better than the Sheyd prince.

John Baltisberger

He stood bemused watching a drunk stumbling down
    the path towards them.
His guard was eager to be on their way, it was almost
    over and done.
They had marched so many miles, and now this
    prisoner wishes to tarry for a drunk?
But Ashmandai stood still, he may not have his
    magical might, but he was a mighty man.

"Not left but right go!
This is the way home for you.
Your wife waits clueless."

The drunk stumbled on thankful for the kindness
for the heavily robed and cloaked stranger
and his captor stared once more amused

"Once again a kindness most surprising
from a demon whose lair was filled
with the bones and skins of men."

Ashmandai could keep silent no more,

"You know nothing, fool!
Of the places I have been;
to judge me so harshly!

You believe me mad?
Or evil, or perhaps not?
Perhaps you don't think.
Would that be easier fool?
If I were merely demon?

War of Dictates

Those I killed were scum.
Wicked to the very core.
Is it not written
'One is allowed to provoke
sinners, and thieves, the wicked?

And so it is now,
that drunken buffoon you saw,
an adulterer, worse
a killer, a wife beater.
I have now led him astray.

He will likely fall
down some stairs, into water
and drown until dead.
Believe I will be rewarded
this I do not for his wife.

But know this, jailor—
in is stated in Heaven
whomever vexes
this man will then have a place,
a home, in the world to come."

His captor, the lariat bearer who strung him along,
    stared in awe
this demon thought it could get a place in the world
    to come
that his murderous rampage would not be the sum of
    all he was worth?
It was not the hunter's duty to judge the beast, only
    to capture until release.

John Baltisberger

The ancient Prince was driven before the young King.
Presented as a sizable prize before Solomon in a court that
glimmered in gold and jewels and greed, from which women
dangled from every angle imaginable.
Solomon wore the ring, for now Ashmandai would serve the king.

The lustful king would sing songs in the morning
before parading his captive in court before courtesans
a slave of Sheydim who contained so much knowledge
of the world passed by, as is, as would come.
Solomon took great pride in depriving the Sheydim of their freedom.
Calling them demons from outside this dimension for reason that
Ashmandai was all too familiar with.

The fully formed humans feared all things differentiated
from their own exhausting existences, exiting all reason
excited to violence for the sake of preserving their own little minds.
And so, the Sheydim in myriad form of half-formed reality
and the dreams of potential for which they could never reach
were the chief of nightmares for mankind whose own kind
should be the nightmares they feared.

War of Dictates

Ashmandai swallowed his relief wallowing in disbelief
at the luck of the book not falling into the hands of
this
power hungry liege of the country of milk, of honey.
Should that have befallen then Solomon's power,
uncommon,
would have moved to the catastrophic challenging
celestial beings bringing an apoplectic Apocalypse
onto mankind for the sins of one grandchild.

Instead he existed in this twisted court lifted from the
future fever dream
of Byzantine empires circled serpentine around sense
Air dense with incense choking the oxygen the
humans needed to survive.
Around them angels danced invisibly a slow waltz of
agony.
Torn between what was good and what was evil in this
hovel of grandeur.
The Sheyd Prince clapped in irons reading patterns
in the smoke of lanterns,
a party trick disguised as blessing guessing at fortunes
for Solomon's guests.
Providing advice without visible price for those who
asked who would later
revel in their revealed scar tissue receipts due at the
butcher for their insolence.
But as with every moment the Sheyd took the long
view of the game.
While humans claimed no shame enjoying the same
diversions from riddle and flame,
he wormed himself like the shamir into Solomon's
ear,

built a veneer of belief around himself like a cloak of smoke that hid his true intentions.

Each day Solomon would ask advice of the wise Ashmandai
looking for answers as to when and why on every matter under the sky
and the Sheyd would answer as Sheydim do honestly but wreathed as they were
in shadow.
Then finally the day came without fanfare or affair while Solomon was unaware,
he asked the question that would set Ashmandai unchained and free as the air.

"The seal of Solomon"

Yes, in his zeal he named it after himself.
This was no new deal but an arrogance Ashmandai had come to expect
from a man who could not detect respect for any other than his own being.
"The seal is powerful it is mighty enough to ensnare ninety demons.
It encompasses the seasons, brings the rains through the control
of your kind, but I feel it could do more, I feel this is a mere steppingstone.
On my path to greatness. How can I increase its control over strangeness?"

"Oh, great Solomon,
whose glory knows no equal
this I can teach you.

War of Dictates

You crafted your seal
in gold and tempered in flame
before breathing spells . . .

Your amulet lacks
the power of the ocean
the power of waves.

Lower your talisman
beneath the surf on the coast
allow the water

to bless it fully
with oceanic presence
then the seal will be

what you meant it be—
as you always intended
to control all things."

He walked bemused beside the ecstatic king,
amused by the boy who saw cookies within reach at last.
They rode side by side guard fanned out behind them
on the way to the shore where Solomon was sure his
    written rights
would ride the waves to reinforced reputation as the
    greatest of sovereigns.
All the while Solomon chided him for not speaking
    sooner.
as though he were a child subject in the presence of a
    stately king
instead of lord of Sheydim amid a toddler's reign.

John Baltisberger

Ashmandai could hardly hold his laughter
as the gullible leader of the chosen people dipped his
seal
under the waters of the sea on the shores of Bat Yam.
He held his shock as one of the Sheydim who
retreated to the deeps
during the flood that had cleansed the earth heeded
Ashmandai's desire
swam close and swallowed the seal whole.

He wanted to laugh.
He intended to laugh.

Ashmandai's rage exploded outward.
A great billowing cloud of sulfur and darkness.
Such was the pent-up frustration of the Lord of the
Half Born
that as he stretched his true form his wings
outstretched shaded the sun—
one tip scratched the deepest earth, the other scraped
the very gates of heaven.
The sudden expansion flung the lustful boy king far away
flinging him like so much useless garbage across the
sands and rivers and lakes
let him make as his forefathers
and trek across the desert subsisting on mana and
crumbs and dew.

As Ashmandai reenacted the created contracting into
himself once more,
he took the face of Solomon, let the Israelites believe
their king was unharmed.

War of Dictates

Believe that he had banished Ashmandai to the dark places and would return
to the place where he sat in opulence.

Ashmandai considered his options in as the screaming subsided.
He could escape this wretched land and be done.
But his freedom was hard won, and now he could take the place of David's son.
What if he took this opportunity, twisted these mortals back to a path?
Where freedom and reason would reign and beget a new era,
breaking free of the shackles of idiotic Grigorim and slave driving Nephilim

Impostor

Imagine taking the place of a ruler not out of greed
but a need to do something right, to set things along
    a more pristine path
would that Ashmandai could set these fragile things
along the steps of a road steeped not only in good
    intention.
Change the impression of the fallen and purge the
    infection
of this thinking from the minds of the population.
He dismissed his courtesans with discretion
    dispersing wealth
to allow for the women's health as he set about to rule
    in stealth.
Solomon's greed had swelled the coffers with tribute
    from far away fathers
paying Israel honors that it had scarcely deserved.

The life of a human king was a different substance
and despite years of living in Solomon's abundance
watching the boy live out indulgence by the dozen.
Had hidden the tedium of human politics and intrigue
    from his eyes.
The mortals were so short sighted they needed to be
    guided

War of Dictates

to answers that common sense would have provided.
They delighted in schemes that were so meaningless,
that Ashmandai felt they had forgotten dreams
replaced passion and screams with base scenes and
grey themes.

He locked himself away for a time, ruling by proxy,
and wrote.
Ironic that his work would always be known
as the words of the man he replaced,
a song of Solomon writ for the land he loathed
and for a Creator who left him unfinished.
But wasn't he now assisting these chosen?
Bending his own path to right the wrongs done by
renegades
rebelling in revolution against that same Creator?
Was he not suppling some form of crutch to the
heavens
to move this world closer to that to come.
His own form of Tikkun Olam for an Olam
that he had been denied by the king of kings?

Ashmandai ignored all of these questions as he
wrote—
wrote words of lust and sex, of adoration and
supplication.
To his beloved locked below the lands littered in limbs
of angel and man,
he harbored no feelings of domination of submission.
There was only the yes and now and no and then,
when she wished to be owned he owned her,
and when she wished to master him she was his
goddess.

John Baltisberger

He poured out his every ounce of emotion into this
    song of psalms
besting anything done by that adulterant pretender
    David.
When he finished, he returned to court, a new chain
    and prison
for him to answer to.

Day in and day out of course Ashmandai listed
    through life
concealing his illicit lack of stimulation with human
    affairs
offering unthinking counsel to bitter little people.
The lies and fabricated reality of citizens conspiring
to block his path to a brighter tomorrow.
He was unable to help the infinitesimally small
    mortals
with their true problems for all the infinitesimally
    small troubles
they brought before him obscured the true goal.

Warily the Sheyd lord opened an eye to observe the
    two woman
who whined and warred before Solomon's visage.
They argued over a human child who even now spit
    and cried
and smelled of shit.
Ashmandai waved a hand unthinking.

"Cut the boy in half.
Each of you may then have part,
is this not perfect?"

War of Dictates

Why was he shocked when one woman agreed?
Why did the court not laugh and jeer at his jest?
Ashmandai rose and approached the two women.
One wailed and begged the guards to step away,
she would relinquish her hold on the boy, give it to
    the other.
While the other seemed unbothered.
Why? Even if she was not the mother, why would she
    applaud the death
of the thing she wanted?

Ashmandai offered a long finger to the child, who
    suckled the proffered digit.
This small creature who held no malice, no trace of
    the poison
that leaked from the wounds the Grigori opened on
    the world.
He was fully formed in a way that Ashmandai's people
    were not.
But at the same time, unformed, a bundle of potential
that could move any way through the world.

He looked at the two women, anger in his own heart
bursting forward. Was he not a father?
Did he not raise his own sons and daughters and others,
watching them raise from bundled potential to fully
    realized people?
And now this thing masquerading as a woman who
    was filled
with the trademark need for property and ownership
that marked his ancient enemy would end the boys
    life,
simply to not lose to the other.

John Baltisberger

He smiled at the child, shushing his cries before
  turning to the women.
Smile falling away he tapped into a voice he had
  hidden for many years.
A voice in tune with the workings of the world and the
  fabric behind reality.

"One of you lies now,
one of you seeks to harm him;
one of you will die."

He didn't know which was truly the mother,
but he would not give it to be another child
who lived as a trophy for its parent.
He would gift the child, right or wrong to the other.
To the one who would protect a young life rather than
  win.

"Dry your tears, mother,
I know you raise him well
with loving kindness."

Lifting the child from bassinet
the demonic king parading as the wise
handed the babe off to the woman who would raise
  him well.

He could feel the other attempting to slip away
but his voice cracked like thunder against the tile of
  the palace.

War of Dictates

"Your cruelty has earned
the coldest winter I have
exiled from this land."

He watched her face now crumble
another's death or loss affected her not
but this moment when she paid the price of not caring
the toll due for her own ineptitude brought her
sorrow.
Ashmandai had no mercy for her.
No kind words or gentle hand.

Humans needed guidance, they needed a firm lead
to take them to the world to come.
And he would drag them if need be
from this place of casual cruelty and hatred of the
unknown.
To show them that a blooming of kindness would
redirect them
from low to highness and succor solace in the heat of
a world
that largely would not care until they all made the
effort to.

Ashmandai was re-resolved in his course when the
palace gates came crashing open.
A beggar stood before them, dirty and worn from
travels across the lands,
dirty and tired and incredibly angry.
Solomon gazed at Ashmandai the pretender
and lifted the Book of the Children high in his hands.

John Baltisberger

Ashmandai let drop the illusion he had wrapped
around himself like the sands that shifted to surround
    the oasis.
He stood in all his glory once more himself in this
    story
discarding the tawdry form of a bawdy king
to face down this new leaner man the child had
    become.

Solomon had been a threat before when his
    knowledge
was contained by earthly things that a man could
    learn.
But now he had the tome written by Ashmandai's
    hand—
The Book of Children—of the dead names of fallen
    things
penned in angelic blood on Nephilim flesh
before being blotted with the breath of dying gods.

It contained knowledge grasped from the air,
received in the moment the sun burst over the
    horizon
and recorded as it died once more for the night.
From the look in his eyes Solomon had studied,
learned the dead names and living flames
could lay claim to the arcane game that stymied
more learned brains and left the weak in chains.

Ashmandai had banished a simpleton and weakling
sent him squealing across the ceiling of the world.
And now he was confronted by the strength that
    hardship had born.

War of Dictates

He swept towards the ragged once-king ready to deal
dread
but was brought up short as the man summoned a
sword of light.
Was this right? Would they now display their might
so basely with a fight?
Would the bright sword cut through the night lord
and sunder the sight of the horde
of Israelites that gathered to observe the confrontation?

Ashmandai stepped back, and summoned his own
weapon,
the spear 'Khofesh' formed in heaven from solidified
questions
crafted in the tension when freedom threatened
order.
Strengthened in the blood of rebellion and tempered
in passion;
a whirling cyclone of death in the service of the
eternal prince.

This Solomon no charlatan at the head of a harlequin
court.
He had divorced himself from the opium of his
utopian courts.
He had left the kingdom a king and returned a man.
Who would return now to his post post-Sheydim.
The ruse was up, what was there to have here in battle
with a mortal man?

A mortal man who sated his lust on so many consorts,
who had imprisoned so many of Ashmandai's
subjects

John Baltisberger

and subjected the Sheyd Prince to imprisonment,
Ashmandai believed not in honor for honors sake,
but he had no small amount of rage to slake against
    the rake of a man.

Like shadows cast by clouds across the sky,
Ashmandai moved forward a funerary shroud
screaming the sound of murderous shouts
echoed in fear by crowds that watched from the sidelines.
The prince assumed this would be over soon—
two strikes and the fallen king would fall again.
The people would keen and wail as his mortal body
    failed.

Khofesh struck the sword of light instead of flesh
Ashmandai had sought to test the fresh meat of the
    man
and now he struggled to hold back his counterpart
a lunge for his heart like a dart of sunlight
glinting against the darkness of the shadowed prince.
The prince spun away from the king's blade
narrowly avoiding being flayed and made to pay
for degrading the disloyal Israeli royal.

Joyful now, the lifted a fist and commanded the wind;
attracted a storm of pressure to lift Ashmandai
to fling Ashmandai as Ashmandai had flung him
across the deserts and into the dangers amongst
    strangers.
Like papers caught in a storm the Sheyd prince was
    tossed
across the royal palace and into the street.
He paused to consider the power.

War of Dictates

Solomon had the book; he had studied it.
Where before he had been a lucky practitioner,
now he had the knowledge to do true damage
access to secrets beyond the scope of what man
    should know.
The prince rose, his wings unfurled to the sky,
half created but fully immortal, fully immersed
in a world that he had never been given in fairness.
He would face down the creator's favored children
of the creator's favorite child.
Did he hold some resentment for his half-brother Adam?
He had stolen his wife, while Adam had stolen his life,
He was no Esau, but his birthright was taken;
wrenched out of socket by the ancestors of Jacob
before ever he had a chance.
Would this blow he struck against Solomon make him
    feel better?
Or was he raging against only the eternal nothingness
of his own nonobjective subjectivity surrounding of
    reality?

Even as he considered this, he watched Solomon step
    from the palace.
Joining him in the sands that would soon be stained
    by one of their blood.
Around them were innocent men and women, who
    stared in fear
abject terror at the fiend in king's robes
facing the haggard beggar who bore the king's face.
Below them the shifting sands of the deserts of Israel,
Ashmandai could harden the sands, making molten
    glass blades

John Baltisberger

that would rain down on Solomon and his people.
Ashmandai raised a hand, boiling the air
summoning the heat of the Nephilim to himself.
But these were people he had strove to save . . .

Humans who had slowly begun turning away from the
   poison
the Gigori had left them as a parting gift.

Ashmandai lowered his hand and gestured with
   Khofesh.
They would settle this in the old way, no gentle mental
   games,
simply metal against mettle and until one bled the
   special life force
down several steps of the temple.

They clashed, light and shadow, a good man and a
   godly being.
Solomon would be no Israel but like Jacob and Adam
   before him,
he would rob Ashmandai of what he strove so hard
   for
again and again, strike to strike, until Ashmandai felt
   a familiar dread.
The seal had him once again.

Cut in his Sheyd flesh the symbols, carved there over
   the course of their clash
unnoticed in the dance of death they had weaved
   across the square.

War of Dictates

"This will not hold me,
my flesh will heal before you,
and I will be free.

I will not be trapped;
your seal won't hold me again!
You have not won this."

Solomon, wiser than ever he was before,
crueler and kinder than he had been,
shook his head and rammed the sword deep into the
    Sheyd.

A sword of light, inscribed with names of angels,
it unmade him, breaking him apart, the Sheyd king,
to his disparate parts, and with it, his dreams of
    healing humankind.

Crusades

(1095 CE—Rhineland Valley)

Deep under the earth in a place called Nod,
east of Eden but west of the known world
the prince of twilight's eyesight restored and
was rewarded
with the image of his bride and with hair like night
whose eyes spoke of the light of passion within her.
She cradled the once dead undying Sheyd in arms
that had held him so many centuries before.
Centuries? No, millennia, ages, eons.

He had not seen her since they had seen the way
Grigorim had twisted her children of a first marriage
into servile things who shunned freedom for ease.
Twisted into shifty weak-willed beings that didn't
understand
the interconnectivity of the light of the world
leaving all things to wither separately together.

Ashmandai had known they would be together again
the same way a perennial knows it will bloom again.
It was only natural that the masterful unilateral love

John Baltisberger

they shared would survive the collateral damage of
   cultural upheaval.
They were as inseparable a pleasureful was to
   vulnerable.
An attraction inexorable and inevitable
bound by impenetrable penetration of bodies
and minds and the heart of the matter had been
   sealed
with whispered words behind Adam's back as the
   days melted into nights
and the moon froze the stars in place as the first
   winters wracked the world.

It was no surprise that as he recovered from
   Solomon's sword
entering him measuring off his lifeline and severing
   his thread.
That his essence would be found sheltering with and
   surrendering to Lilith.

"I wrote poetry
under the guise of a man,
in your name, Lilith."

She smiled down at the man in her lap.
He was almost enough to make her forget the terrible
   mess
that the once-divine things had made of her human
   once-family.
Almost.

"I read it dear, Ashmand, I read the words you wrote
as you pretended at a lesser crown. Trying to right

94

wrongs that you didn't commit, and I know you
do these things for me."

He rose from her lap and turned the attention of his
    lips
to rediscovering her skin once again desperate to taste
    her.
She did not shy away from his kisses, providing no
    chase.
But he was not some idiot who demanded a game.
He wasted no haste wrapping up her waist and
    pulling her close.
But still she pressed three fingers to his lips as he
    moved forward to sample hers.

"You are still far too weak to satisfy me,
even with all the rest you've had,
but it has been the age of the world since
I have felt you have filled me, and I would have that
    again
no matter how briefly.
You wrote such pretty words,
I hope it is not all your tongue and hands are good for
    now?"

Ashmandai smiled at the challenge laid before him.
He was weak in body, but not in enthusiasm,
and Lilith's body was one he had explored so
    frequently
that even in the long years of a million missed
    moments
he could close his eyes and remember every smooth
    curve

and loved mark on her skin.
He had traced her stretch marks and worshiped at the alter
of her appearance at every stage they had spent together.
He was more familiar with the caress of her touch than
his own body, even after all this time.

Even armed with this knowledge Ashmandai took his time.
He touched every spot as though it was the first instance
of intimacy between them.
Acting as lovers when they first overcome fear to stand before
each other as once they did in the garden of paradise.
He spent his dreams into her.
Long years of longing for her taste on his tongue.
And now he couldn't resist touching every softness and hardness to her.
And buried his face in her to meet with her demands of pleasure.
The Sheyd do not need to breath as humans, and he used this to her advantage.

When she could bear no more foreplay,
when his tongue and hands were no longer enough
and she needed to feel his weight above her she pulled him up and over her body.
She was no shy woman who would make her lover guess what she wanted.
With hands made soft caressing his hair as he healed

she guided him into her and wrapped her legs about
    to squeeze.
Pushing him further and harder than either were
    ready for.
The pain of new penetration after eons without made
    her gasp.
They were not gentle in their sex, but tenderness of
    emotion
met the feral passion they displayed to combine in
    archetype of love
that humans would try to emulate throughout their
    short lives.

In quick succession they would meet and fuck and
    separate
mere inches, as far as they were willing to part
and as soon as he recovered, they came back again
to cum together again, spurning and pleasures
other than the other for another forty days and forty
    nights.

The very earth east of Eden shook as he pounded into
    her
as she thrust against him, until their imagination and
    his body
gave out and not a moment before.
They fell apart panting, their needs met
for a moment, but not sated.

But while they had waited
this was not why she had woken him she stated.

John Baltisberger

"The world is a bloody place,
bloodier since you last walked
the planes and places of shadows and men.
The children of Adam are dying . . . "

Ashmandai turned to her, admiring the way
that sweat gleamed in the low light of their
hidden fortress deep in the earth.

"Let them die, my love.
They have not done aught for us.
Their greed drives them on."

Lilith pulled her man's chin up, meeting his black eyes
with orbs that blazed with the brilliance of the Borealis.
Cold as the depths of space but filled with the fury no
    tsunami could match.

"Do not be flippant, Adam's children are mine as well.
Dismiss my past and you dismiss a part of me,
would you be so glib as to do away with that?"

Ashmandai had the decency to look ashamed,
what was important to the one he clung to was
    important to him.
He hung his head and stilled his tongue, her words
    stung in the truth of what he had done.
Forgotten his place by her side.
She watched the half born with full love in her heart.
Her passion, love, and anger equal measure an anchor
    he could dock
his fleeting reality to as he recalibrated and
    reconstituted himself.

War of Dictates

But she no longer had time to wait and be gentle with
  him.
He was her husband and thus the father of her
  children, his and otherwise.

Her wrath could be terrible, the continuing
  perversion of humankind;
the poison that slithered its way through mankind
  would spurn her towards destruction.
An explosion of a mother's rage at the loss of
  innocence
that shattered the world into countless darkening
  shards of pain.

"My children and Eve's children suffer at the hands
  of angels once again.
The oldest enemy of mankind's poison and greed
  speeds their creed
towards obliteration of the other that is no other . . .
So, go Ashmandai, be my vengeance and wrath.
Steer humanity back on course towards being a force
  of freedom."

Ashmandai, reborn anew after two thousand years of
  oblivion,
left the earth east of Nod to defend humanity once
  again from itself.

Insanity was a scent that carried on the air,
a tangible fungus throwing spores and growing wars.
Fermenting zealotry amongst peasantry given agency
by painfully and blatantly corrupted priests.
Hermits that were degenerates carrying forged documents

disgorged armies of unwashed Christians to topple
monuments.
Disguising their purpose towards preparation the
congregation made a pact.
Following the foul fowl to find Emicho and join in his
deadly cause.
Why travel across the treacherous lands of sand and
Muslims
when there were Jews here to ventilate?
Enough to satiate the great hunger for violence in the
men.
This was never about a holy land. Only a need to replay
old wars and violence, giving way to old ways
Taught in the angelic towers of the first city of
Grirgorim.
The tide of sweat rusted armor and too-dull swords
swarmed
like ants that tore at the very flesh of the world.
Ripping the veneer of life and comfort away from the
decayed corpse
of rotten meat and bulbous flies the earth had
become.
There in the Rhine amongst the old country wine and
swine
the daily grind ground to a halt by columns of cross
wearing charlatans
bearing swords and axes beaten from plowshares to
take their share
of property from those they had decided didn't count
as human.
Those that would convert they subverted to their cult.
New soldiers forced to kill their fathers, too old to be
useful.

War of Dictates

Forced to torture mothers or be tortured themselves.
Starting on the edge and working inward swinging swords
made bloody with innocent blood they called heretical.
Hysterical wherewithal swept those whose houses had not yet been raided;
slid knives across throats mothers killing babes as father's;
slaughtered their children by way of a single knife stroke
across the veins, vainly attempting to send their children off
before the shadow of the cross fell across their doors.
Mothers having killed children,6 husbands murdered wives.
And with the last ounce of strength pulled the twine taunt
cutting themselves off from the monsters that stalked the earth.

Moshe Ben Avraham kneeled in the dirt with his congregation.
The occupation of the Rhine valley had come with no provocation,
the complete domination that followed the confrontation—
no condemnation from priest or pope could slow their greed.
They fed like rats feed deaf to human pleas as they glutted on
meat of what was once the Rhine.

John Baltisberger

One by one they took the men before a priest who
    made the offer;
join Yeshua's cult or be sent to death.
Tears stream down faces worn with age and honest
    work.
Old men whose hands had trembled while ending
    their kin
who were not swift enough in leaving this world and
    would now
wave the world taken away on cruel Christian terms.
Moshe realized there was another man kneeling next
    to him.
His knees pressed into the blood-soaked mud
congealing into scabs that glued them in place in the
    horror
that every new hour introduced to be induced into the
ruined psyche of the Jewish people of the Rhine.

"Can you speak the Sh'ma, brother?"

Moshe's voice was a broken thing
rasping through bloodied dirt caked lips
with a breath that had already whispered so many
    prayers
that fell on deaf ears that there was hardly breath left
to utter the dead words to dead worlds
that would accept the dead of the Rhine Valley.
The stranger who kneeled beside him only shook his
    head.

"No need to pray now,
the unheard words won't help you.
But I intend to."

War of Dictates

Moshe looked down; head bowed by the obvious madness
that touched his new friend.
Madness was nothing new on this day,
men forced to kill their families before being killed
before the weeping visage of these invader's cruel god.
The soldiers approached again, ready to condemn again
ready to kill a man again and bathe in the sin of bloodshed again.
They pulled the stranger to his feet, spitting words of their "Christ" in his face.o
so enraptured in the power they found in their hate.
The way their sound bounced off walls and ground to echo
in the face of their prey that they had tunnel vision drowned
in the profound darkness of over confidence and did not notice,
he was unbound.

The stranger dissipated which instigated surprised shouts
from the guards who investigated his whereabouts
being manipulated by sophisticated magic enacted
by the king that had never walked the Earth on human feet.
The soldiers unwittingly breathed in the smoke the Sheyd had become.
When he rematerialized, they realized their life was trivialized,
their demise so sudden as Ashmandai ripped their lungs from gaping mouths

John Baltisberger

that found themselves so suddenly filled with blood
and inhuman flesh.

A hot wind blew across the town as the prince flapped
his wings.
Singeing the eyes of those who stared in shock with
each lantern extinguished.
The clouds obscured the moon, hiding the killing
fields and bloodstained shields.
The only light left was the blaze set to Jewish homes
and the synagogue.
Crusaders trembled as the fires of the temple stoked
by their hate sputtered
and died as fully as the victims they had already
claimed that night.
Men's minds were not set to take the mental strain of
what they saw.
No illusion of humanity held in Ashmandai. Simply a
brutality punctuated by enmity
and the sanctity of the murder he set himself to.
In the darkness his eyes raged with black flames on
the back of the black starless night.
As graceful as an angel, as cruel as the monsters that
he had set himself against eons ago,
he moved through the town taking the crusaders to
task for crimes committed here.
Their blood would meld with that of the chosen they
had slaughtered like pigs.
Not even the Creator would be able to sort the flesh
rent from bone by the king.

That night lasted years, for some in excruciating
agony.

War of Dictates

Others huddled under beds listening to those that the
half-born found.
He bore into their flesh with claws grown from the
sorrow and timeless resentment.
Ashmandai unbound beheld his handwork, he had
excelled—
the broken bodies of Christian invaders lay strewn
across the Rhine.
His work was unfinished, Emicho must die or the
horde would rise again.

Follow the sound of the ripping, gore dripping from
the rafters, slipping down
into puddles of crimson flood waters that washed
decency away.
Ashmandai entered the synagogue to find the
orchestrator of the carnage he had joined.
His hands were painted red, he barely recognized his
own monstrous visage
in the warped thing reflected in the deep pools of
blood that oozed past.

Emicho was hunched over Moshe ben Avraham,
a hand gripping the meat under each lip as he peeled
the flesh from the still living skull,
the screams absorbed by the thick liquid coating the
house of worship.
This was the man who led the rabble, who touted the
bible
as the inciting force of violence, forcing destruction
on the creation
of the Creator in their name as though the two things
were the same.

John Baltisberger

Emicho was a swollen thing, his girth barely kept in
   check
by the armor he wore, the chains that lashed it to him
digging deep gashes in his flesh where fat and blood
   welled from the wounds.
Wounds that the psychotic Crusader lord did not notice.
So intent was he on the work of peeling the Rebbe's
   face from the curvature of his bones
that he did not realize he was not alone.

But Ashmandai knew this polluted soul, no matter
   what vessel it wore.
He had last left the violent vile villain lashed to the
   bottom of a mountain
in a villa of nothingness in deepest Sheol where Enoch
   had left him.
How a Grigori could be here summoning a tide of gore
spreading across the floor to swallow their legs to
   their knees
Ashmandai did not know.
But he did know that this thing had left its prison
   throne
to enact a bloody vengeance on the lineage of Enoch
from Rhine to holy shrine in holy land leaving holes
   in the land
filled with the bodies of holy men.

"Hello little half prince."

The voice that rumbled from the grotesque Emicho
gargled through a trachea that was flooded with
   human offal.

War of Dictates

Hardly discernable as words but whose meaning was clear—
clear as the death of the Rebbe, his constituent parts had come apart
and now floated in the river of Emicho's making down the waterfall of the Bimah.

"Azazel reborn,
a sack of meat filled with hate,
war's lost scholar"

Ashmandai had a special hate in his heart for this bastard fallen.
He was no common, rotten thug who wallowed in the debasement of humans
but a philosopher king who reigned in a theology of violent ideology.
A professor of violent psychopathy teaching his progeny the ways
of war's technology and murder's biology seeping in his special brand of pathology
like a pathogen that infected humanity to its core.
Leaving a race who ever sought to even the score in never ending war.

The bloated dead man housing the will of a shard of creation chuckled.
A wet sound that sounded off the walls echoing in the hearts of men
across the world who suddenly rose up to take up arms and kill their brothers.
Azazel-Emicho turned, the sputtering torches glinting of the oily fat

John Baltisberger

that pushed up around the chains burrowed into his
     flesh.

"Not so lost, not where you could not find me. Found
     me.
Left me. You are not a particularly good ally,
     Ahsmandai; false friend.
Begin to understand, that we waited and thought you
     would bring salvation,
but we are the watchers and we watched.
We watched as you led Og astray, watched you
     butcher him where he lay.
We watched you betray us little Sheyd. And we could
     wait no longer.
We could watch no longer. You wish to make war on
     us as prisoners.
Now you will have war amongst your home, amongst
     the children
of your whore wife, and the strife we bring will be like
     a knife
that strikes against the life of your own children.
You will bleed as we have bled. You will die as we have
     died.
You will suffer in ways that none have suffered
     before."

"You count victory
before we can even fight
I am not idle.

While you chewed your chains;
while you screamed into the void,
I have marshaled strength.

War of Dictates

You have remained weak,
where I have grown in stature.
Your rebellion ends."

The watcher bent over in mirth, his posture creating
    a monster
in the shadows on the wall which only paled in
    comparison
to the author of the carnage of the Rhine.

"Do you think I care, even a little
for what land these foolish flesh sheaths consider
    holy?"
Azazel-Emicho reached into the gore to retrieve a
    tongue
floating free of skull in a coagulating pond of pain.
He ran his own tongue, bloated and squirming with
celestial parasites across the other appendage,
a gentle caress like a kiss for the violated dead
before he tore into it with teeth broken from cracking
    bone
slurping the meat of the words of man down into an
    already filled vessel.

"You have lost your book, and with the letters you
    have written in the blood
of our kind, with the skin of our offspring, with the
    words of things older than creation.
We will take the power we want and tear all of
    creation apart, to remake it anew
in an image pleasing to us in which we are the gods
    man deserves and the author of the old

John Baltisberger

is chained in place to a place that is no place and
    nothing but the endless ending will be their
    companion."

Revealing his plan Azazel smiled, a scythe of blood
    forming from the death
to be wielded by the red horseman on this and on the
    last day.
"You are half-born and half powered, immortal
    maybe, but only because they have forgotten you.
But I have not little Sheyd, and on this day, in this
    place, I will delight in sending you broken
back to your whore for another century."

The two immortals clashed in the house of prayer,
one slayer the other protector.
Born of simpler times
which they themselves complicated;
turned the white and black of day and night,
grey with muddled blood splatters against the horrified
    sight
of dead eyes whose eyelids at been ripped off
by eager teeth prior to the fight,
a mute choir of an audience to witness Azazel's delight.
The angel had no time for fair fights or honor or
    proving.
He delved deep into the throws of violence.
He loved war for the scale of the substance but found
    excellence
in even the turbulence of a man striking his wife for
    insolence.
Any evidence of the violence was enough to bring
    Azazel

to attention and ready for action of the unwilling flesh
    of partners
that would never survive his tender administrations.
His caresses were always closed fists on the unbruised
    skin
so he could watch it bloom, and then remove it
to hang in the gallery of his victories.

As the human crusaders were to the Sheyd prince,
Ashmandai was to Azazel, a child before a titan,
a rag doll thrown about the synagogue without effort.
If he had human bones to break, they would have
    shattered,
bursting from skin like so much shrapnel
to leave tatters of ruined flesh behind that would
    never heal or be worn again.
If Ashmandai was human.
Once he had screamed to the heavens in rage about
    not being made whole,
about being a half-created thing, an unfinished king
wallowing on the workbench of creation.
He had held resentment until Lilith melted it away
and from that day he had never again desired
    humanity.
Immortality offered the chance to spend eternity
with and in her eternally stretching into infinity.

Now Ashmandai wished for mortality again.
For all his unnatural bulk, a meat suit grown on sweet
    fruits
and candied swine moved as fast as time
faster than the prince could react in his weakened
    state.

John Baltisberger

The Watcher toyed with him, sloshing through the
   bloody Rubicon
to catch the prince and reach inside, his fingers
   parting flesh
blunt tips forcing their way in the bloody mess and
   ruin
of Ashmandai's body to grab ribs and break them off.
Pull them out of his body with a whip crack of abused
   meat
and wave the shattered bone like batons.
The angel used the sheyd's bones as shanks, crafting
   new holes
in the skin of the immortal victim.

"Forget the whore! Let me make you a new woman.
She can be the half-born's half whore, and you can
   frolic
in a garden I make for you from the bones of Yakov's
   grave."

Torn asunder and body plundered, ravaged of bone,
   strength and will.
Ashmandai could not die and escape the twisted joy
   of the twisted angel.
He became smoke and Azazel inhaled him, mixing
   him with gore streaked phlegm
before spitting him out as steaming bloody snot.
He phased through walls and Azazel followed
   knocking walls down.
There was no peace or escape from the Watcher who
   watched his tricks
close enough to catch each one and counter it with
   single minded delight.

War of Dictates

"You are hoping I grow bored, but I have dreamed of
    the delights we will share.
I have spent entire earthly empires designing
    violations just for you."

Ashmandai panted crawling towards the entry of the
    synagogue.
His breath came out in heavy gasps pulling air into
    torn lungs
that refused to inflate when so full of rasping holes.
With each exhalation, Ashmandai left more of himself
    behind.
Each dragged inch a titanic effort to stay corporeal
    another second.

When Azazel reached the stricken Sheyd again
he reached out and was amazed when his hands
    grasped nothing.
Little by little Ashmandai had released bits of his
    essence,
dripping down into the blood-soaked floor and earth.
sinking lower until there was too little left
for even the Grigori to grasp.

Azazel roared his rage at the prince's escape.
But his roars were as impotent as they had been
when he had been a captive.

Ashmandai sunk below the earth, far below those
    darkest places
until he found his home east of Nod.

John Baltisberger

Ashmandai opened eyes sealed shut by bloody tears
breaking the coagulated coating to see into the
    darkness,
his full bodied lover sat before him,
radiant as the moon on the clear night,
luminescent against the dark of their sunken home.
She gazed at him with eyes like pools of dark wine
poured into chalices of crystal for a last supper.
He had failed her so spectacularly, spirit crushed
    utterly.
The angel had been singularly powerful and
    particularly brutal.
but Lilith watched him with the motherly love for a
    father.
His unearthly shame absurdly heightened by how
    unworthy he felt.
To gaze so hungrily upon her splendid form.
But there was no judgment in her eyes or hunger
    either,
something else lived there.

In the long years Ashmandai had reconstituted
his wife had not been idle.
Taking his children, the half-born daemons of
twilight nightmares half formed by the creator
and then finished by the Sheyd's dreams.
These things followed their mother's guiding hand
disguised in the foreign land of Hungary
where they ripped apart Emicho's horde
as a horde of rage themselves.

Again and again as Ashmandai slept staving off death,
his children went into the world of men

leaving the comfort of their dark places and holy
 spaces.
Fighting and dying for the children of Adam who paid
 them no mind.
But Ashmandai and Lilith's code was instilled in the
 essence
of each Sheyd child, their lungs filled with the very
 notion of freedom.
Freedom for all, or freedom for none. The half-
 begotten
have begotten a race of sheydim that would not be
 seen
to sit quietly while the despoiled race of fallen angels
wiped their ass with the remnants of their human
 cousins.

Azazel had faced the queen of Sheydim and tried to
 abuse her as he had her lover.
Her rage empowered her in a way the jovial Azazel
 was unprepared for,
but in the center of a war, where his men idolized him,
he was at the seat of his power, and in that hour, he
 would not be crushed
by the stuck up first wife of the first insufficient man.
His force was routed, and he took that anger out on
 Lilith—
each punch thrown and claw swiped a crushing blow
 of untold strength.
Two titans that caused the earth to shake as they bellowed
in eons old hate at one another, toppling homes and
 churches
with a fight that could not be won by either primordial
 force.

John Baltisberger

Only as he was surrounded by the legion of shadow-
   children
the loyal get of the disloyal prince did he relent.
He could have killer her; her immortality was not
   indestructible.
She would tire where he would not be surrounded by
   the violent prayers.
But now surrounded entirely by those whose hostility
   was aimed only at him.
Azazel fled abandoning his mortal followers to unkind
   mercy of the Sheydim.

Still, Azazel wouldn't abandon his crusade,
   whispering mad words of holy lands
and plans to elevate their corpse deity's holdings to
   include the land of his bris-milah.
He spoke in fevered dreams to dying popes, planting
   seeds in diseased brains.
And the 'spiritual leaders' who grew fat on the pain of
   the people
who planted their own seeds in the fields of cousins
   and children
frothed at the mouth at visions of a land subsumed by
   the foreskin
of a long dead savior;
a land that continued to be caked with the blood
of all who walked it since the first murder.

The next crusade would just as bloody—
followers of Rudolph the mad flocked to banners of skin
painted with sigils of hate and holy mockery.
The flesh-pennants stiff with human effluvia
did not flap in the wind but oozed stiffly in place.

War of Dictates

Azazel wearing the starved form of the monk was thin
    in the first days,
a starved corpse surrounding the sick light of the
    hateful angel.
He would grow, as Emicho had.
As the angel stuffed his gullet with the corpses of his
    foes.
As he drank in the blood of war and danced with
    lovers
stitched together from victims and warriors who slew
    each other.
With each sexual volatile manifestation of his
    violation of their forms
he would swell like a bladder filling with poisoned piss.

Ashmandai rose from the dark places under the earth
    once more.
He didn't need a word from his bride from the garden,
for he knew his duty was not finished yet,
While the virulent violent villain vacationed in human
    lands.
Azazel, for the good of all creation must be re-interred
under the world, under the mountain, or else the
    fountain
of bloodshed would go un-ended and humanity,
sweet humanity would find itself on its deathbed.

To the Rhine, to Worms to Cologne and to Speyer
the carnage was so widespread.
The emaciated prophet of war whispered words
of frothing frenzy to fetid brains steeped in self-
    righteous vainglory

spilling blood of whomever stepped in their way
towards the path to the holy land that held the unholy
text.
Ashmandai hunted through the waves of brainwashed
soldiers
intoxicated by the promise of forgiven sin and
paradise at the end.
Rudolf, the meat-mask of Azazel, preached
through blackened teeth of the stingy Jew who held
profit askew
keeping the funds needed to wage holy war for
themselves.
From his throne of bone and ash in Mainz.

There Ashmandai whispered words to their saints and
preachers,
undermining the hate with new ideals and ideas.
Worming his will throughout the weakened minds to
depose
aligned more closely than the alien angel turned
demon.
Through reason pushed into subconscious craniums
Ashmandai exerted his subtly in sublime subterfuge.
Redirecting holy fervor indirectly influencing holy
hierarchy
until Randolf's teeth were all pulled, and Ashmandai
could go home,
though no battle-won and Azazel unbowed, the war
would go on.

Over the centuries from that battle Ashmandai toiled,
waging a war unending through centuries of hateful
detritus

War of Dictates

left in the wake of free and vengeful watchers
watching from in between human flocks
who flocked to the would-be gods who offered the
easy road
of self-glorification at the cost of subjugation of the
other.
From Prague to Central America, wherever the many
eyes
of the angels from under the mountain rose—
Ashmandai rose with them, bringing his army.
And the toll was immense.

Human lives thrown away like so much water from a
chamber pot.
Tossed into the streets of history to wash away
unremembered.
Sheydim died though in smaller numbers, ripped
apart
by empowered magi, wielding knowledge Ashmandai
himself had gathered.
The Grigori waged their war against all mankind,
reserving a special hatred for the sons and daughters
of Jacob.
Azazel was chief among them, teaching men wars of
lies and misinformation
trading in superiority and lessening the strength of
unity.

Ashmandai planned in damp caverns with his council,
Lilith by his side.
This was a war they could not win.
This was a battle against a sin inked into the skin of
their human kin,

John Baltisberger

a tattoo so deep it was etched on bone to give power
to the Grigori.
Only through freeing mankind and peeling the
parasitic ink
from their masochistic bones and end the mythic
threat
that loomed from the shadows of history to the
present day.
Enlighten humanity, awaken them to a truth buried
so deep and dark under the colossal offal tower of
excrement
that none knew it existed any longer.
This war could not be fought against the angelic slave-
masters.
It had to be fought against the nature the heaven-
borne scum
had poisoned humanity with.

War of Dictates

(1348 CE—2020 CE)

Plagued

(France/Germany 1348 CE)

Bezaliel and Kokabiel the deceiver who delighted in honeyed words and passed blame

surfaced on the waters of the Riviera, driving before them rats and lies.

Bezaliel lord of the flies that laid eggs in the plentiful corpses

his fleas had carried affliction to throughout Europe.

He played a flute made of a femur that attached to dreams,

awoke men with screams where they would notice a new bite—

a mandible kiss added to the rest that when connected like constellations

spelled the boil pocked death knell and the count swelled.

Kokabiel, lord of lies followed after passing blame from one to another.

John Baltisberger

Mothers watching husbands with mistrust as sisters
    drowned brothers
for playing with rats in the gutters where their
    younger siblings lay rotting.
Kokabiel sang his dirge to Bezaliel's tune, an
    infestation of thought and body.
Sickening mankind as the Watchers always had.

The words spread as fast as the fleas, leaping from
    host to host
sinking in parasite teeth, injecting venomous
    philosophy with every nip.
Here was the Jew, they whispered, who seems
    immune to sickness.
Here is the Jew, they spat, who refuse to drink from
    the well.
Here is the Jew, they roared, who wash their dead and
    defy death!
The chant went from thought to throat each note of
    the song,
a death warrant wrote as the flames of fear's fire grew.
Soon a raging paranoia of a people plagued spread
    prosecution
slaughtering their neighbors in Toulon.
The blood flowed in the open air attracting more
    biting flies
and ravenous vermin who feasted on fallen flesh.
The angelic minstrels followed the red soaked road
obscured in a cloud of flies so dense it blotted out hope.
The twins of disease and deceit hand in hand swept
    the land
carrying with them the pestilential stench of pogroms
    perpetuated

War of Dictates

by presumptuous ignoramuses as they frolicked west
to Germany.

There in Strasbourg they found a citizenry on the
brink of collapse.
Rage at the rich rested firmly on the wretched runts
of Azazel's ire.
The rising fumes of plague fulminated the
propagation of action.
Treaties broken with treacherous treason towards
decency
as the gates of hell opened allowing the citizens of
Stasbourg,
entry into the ghetto, with the angelic watchers at
their head.
Kakabiel cackled and chortled commanding the
catholic crowd
to new heights of prejudiced volcanic panic
driving forward drastic traumatic action and the
flames roared again.
The pits were filled, the ashes of those that died of
Bezaliel's kiss
coated the vital victims of Kakabiel's hissing lies.
The Jews of Stasbourg were set to torch, burned with
pitch and licked with pain.
The twin Watchers watched and pulled the women
who pricked their pricks' fancy.
Over the course of six days the singing and dancing of
hate and pain continued
a bacchanalian celebration for the avatars of diseased
paranoia
illuminated by the two thousand living pyres that had
been honest citizens.

John Baltisberger

Ashes rained down on the murderers, too busy looting the rings
and goods of those whose remains remained like storm clouds in the sky.

As the siblings left the town, they were followed by an unnatural darkness.
A storm of rage that landed miles outside Strasbourg.
Ashmandai stood, high and imperial, the full king of the half-born.
Wings that coated the sky in the blackness of the unformed void
spread behind him like the tapestry of an unknowable future.
In Strasbourg these two were surrounded by pain and worship,
at the height of power, as Azazel had been three centuries past.
Here separated from their flock he would confront them.
In his left hand he wielded the shaft of shadows known as Khofesh.
Still as a statue in the darkness, the three immortals let the moment linger.

"Little shadow, you finally come to join the fun,"
Bazaliel rasped enraptured in possibility.
"You could not take Azazel alone, and yet here you walk,
against not one but two, united in purpose, alone. Alone to die."

War of Dictates

"I fell to him true,
in the place of his power
when I was alone.

But this was folly
it was my painful mistake
not one to repeat."

From behind Ashmandai's wing stepped another—
a dark man with black eyes and robes of deep violet.
He was inviolate in demeanor, and roped of rage
dripped off him like a leper shedding skin.
Kamdiel held in his hand the black blade named
    HaSatan,
the absolute judgment of the Creator.

Kakabiel's smile never left, the mortis grin pulling at
    his skin
though his face stretched in unnatural proportion
forced into rictus by the sight of his brother.
"You bring the Adversary, the prosecutor of all?
You judge the little ones, Kamdiel, not your own."

The response came from all around, echoed in every
    molecule of air
without the use of lips as the manifested unfallen
    spoke with spite.
"You drag them down, you take away the will, yet I am
    not your jailer,
I am not the easy kindness of humans or weakness of
    the sentimental.
I am not the brother you failed to tempt at the
    beginning.

John Baltisberger

In this moment of human suffering, I will not repeat
 Enoch's folly."

Bazaliel formed a scythe of sickly bones, grown from
 the
twisted spines of those who died writhing in the
 suffering
caused by the myriad diseases that blossomed in his
 wake.
Kakabiel had no weapon to wield but words that
 warped
the world around him to weaponize reality itself.

Ashmandai's wings came crashing down in revelation
an army of shadows, the Sheydim gathered under his
 standard,
each half-born answered the call to heal the shattered
 psyche of a scattered people
and imp gripped the twisted shofar and blew a note
 that fractured the air
sending the legion of shadows forward to war . . .

More than two thousand Sheyd died that day,
even separated from power the monsters were
 monstrously powerful
Bazaliel's bladed dance reaped life with every swing,
the bloated lord of congealed rot revealed a concealed
 grace,
and with each fetid step a method to madness that
 swept away his foes.
The fields were filled with the killed sporting spilled
 entrails in the filth
that Bazaliel left behind in his pirouettes.

War of Dictates

The tide of shadow ebbed and flowed across the land,
smashing itself against the twins, the shouted magic
    of Kakabiel
flensed the shadows from the darkened bones,
sending souls into the unknown even as more
    Sheydim
rushed in to replace the dead.

But as powerful as the two were combined, the might
    of the army
backed by the black blade of the Adversary was mightier
they would be taught a lesson in humility with their
    senior brother as teacher,
weaver through the battle to cut deeper and meaner
    into the meager flesh of lesser angels.
Kamdiel bent the plague king over his knee, bending
    spine almost toe snapping
and buried HaSatan in the watcher's chest.
Bazaliel bubbled his bloated flesh boiling in protested
    brayed screams.
Around the wound his flesh peeled back recoiling
    from the kiss of Judgement,
from the gash poured maggots and fleas, a rat
    scrabbled from under ribs.
Bloated as its host on the still living flesh.
But Bazaliel would not be ended so ignominiously,
with a belch he released himself, millions of flies
    flying forth
from between rotten teeth to coat the twilight sky and
    dissipate
once more dissolute into atmosphere to distribute his
    final gifts.

John Baltisberger

The empty husk of his host left to bake in Kamdiel's
   rage.

Alone Kakabiel screamed as his brother's body
   steamed.
The fiend muttered faster words that reshaped matter
throwing wall and flame and pain and death at the
   tidal wave
of Sheyd flesh that engulfed him. To follow his
   brother and lose form,
would mean centuries of work undone a war left not
   won
when mankind was so close to succumbing to their
   final death.
But with Khofesh and HaSatan at his throat the Voice
   of Deciet
had little choice but to beat a retreat, and the cry of
   his escape
tore a hole through the line of Sheyd, slaughtering as
   many of the half-born
as he could take with him into the nether of non-
   existence.

Ashmandai look over the carnage wrought,
was this war well fought? Did it mean a victory had
   been bought?
He turned this thought over in his head as Kamdiel
   wordless left.
Never again would he spend his people's lives so cheaply.
Though each was half soul, half existence, they were
   of full worth to their king.
He fought a war for mankind in the shadows of the
   pain they themselves caused.

War of Dictates

Should he go against the powers when the powers of
    the Creator
ignored the creations pain?
Lilith waited for the triumphant return,
but there would be no fanfare as the dead and dying
    were carried home.
To be buried with honors East of Nod.

Uncivil

(United States 4-9-1865 CE)

The mirror in the tent told lies to the shaving general,
reflecting the skin-deep visage of a man beaten down
by the war between brothers over the freedom of
  others.
Broken by the lack of sleep and the worm-eaten
  rations
that fed him and his men as the Yankees attacked
  again and again.
In truth the thing wearing Edward Alexander's skin
  was jubilant.
The land was fed by the blood of the weak as human
  forced human
to work through crops week after week
until their bones were meals for carrion eaters in
  fields.
This war was a war to keep humans as pets and
  livestock, but not
as the weak Lee or Davis imagined. There was no
  difference between
these white simpletons and those they kept as
  property and in poverty.
It was a puppet show mockery of the earthly barbarity.

War of Dictates

The Grigori owned humanity.
Yeqon, second in falling in following Azazel and
    Semyaza, was invigorated
filled with strength at the suffering all around, the
    conflict filled him.
The war could go on and on and tear the young
    country apart into tiny territories
teeming with self-important warlords who would
    squabble and quibble
and keep repressing the other for the sake of each
    day's convenience.
With the proper encouragement, America could be
    the kingdom of the Watchers;
a nation of Babel risen from the ashes of humans' own
    poisoned psyches.

Then Yeqon was not alone, in the tent before him was
    no man,
no angel, no demon, no half-born six-fingered king.
It wore the shape of a warrior, blue robed like the
    human union
standing out in stark contrast to the drab grays Yeqon
    was forced to adopt.
The Watcher stopped and dropped his razor,
    watching as he did
the man-thing did not attack nor move,
though surely an assassin left bereft of compassion
    sent to fasten
a noose around Yeqon's throat like a medallion of dishonor
for his improper use of human bodies for partners.
He was taller than most, wider than most
radiated a power he could boast as he posed there
    exposed by the tent post.

John Baltisberger

Did he suppose he could impose a challenge and
   depose a Watcher?
By why send a servant? Was he not urgent enough to
   warrant
a visit from the fervent merchant of vengeance?
He had expected to see Ashmandai trailing a
   hopelessly loyal angel.
But no sibling accompanied this lost Sheyd soul, this
   sacrificial lamb
on the altar of Yeqon's power.

"I was expecting someone other,
a wonder you are brave enough to suffer here little
   brother,
you come to face me in my own element beside my
   own regiment.
A testament to bravery, but it means excrement. You
   see,
you come to your detriment; death is eminent my
   elegant impediment."

The Sheyd did not move, regarding the angel with
   sunken red eyes,
the more he was observed the less human he appeared,
like a blackened falcon with scales coiled for action
a serpent poised to strike with violent passion
this assassin from East of Nod, Bel the last dragon.
Having identified the menace that pretended to be a
   nemesis,
Yeqon wasted no time but barreled forward with
   prejudice,
landing kicks and punches into the swiftly evolving bulk
of Bel, the last dragon.

War of Dictates

The two grew, invisible to men's eyes.
grappling and changing over a battlefield
of grays and blues and bloody hues as men were
  pinned
by bayonets and skewered by bullets let fly blindly.
Bel was the mightiest of the Sheydim,
the strength of legend powering his wings,
muscles built on folklore and powered by belief.
The two giants shook the earth unnoticed in the war
  beneath.
But the dragon could not exceed the power of the
  angel
who secreted hate and dominance over all that was
  painful
for hours they fought above the battle zone.
But the undivine had stamina that did not wane
powered by his own lust for the profane and his very
  name
he had struggled against the chains of the Creator
to Yeqon this was a simple game, one that would end
  the same
as every battle against the Watchers had since their
  first reign.

And so fell Bel, the last dragon, down to war stained
  ground.
Dirtied with the deeds of the moment when men no
  longer
allow conscious thought to govern their moment.
They foment violence against the continent,
a punishment for the compliment of saying
that men may be equal, a disfigurement to ego.

John Baltisberger

Brought low by blows to the soul and form,
the would-be assassin would be a companion to Samiel no more.
Yeqon straddled the Sheyd tearing chunks of quivering meat
from the beast, invisible blood fell like tear-salt rain over the plain
where men died and killed in the hundreds to stay enslaved to the Watchers.
In ignorance they died with eyes closed to the truth, and so too did Yeqon
blind Bel as well, thumbs slipped into eye sockets pulping the meat to jelly.
Licking at the mass that squeezed out in sweet victory. But laughter made him stop.
The birth of mirth blasted from the gore stained teeth of the unseen dragon.
Boiling blood bubbling with the wheezed cackle that crackled through Yeqon's hide.

"Know little angel that fell from so high, that this place will be your loss.
You think I was an assassin deceived, who believed I could kill you?
Do you not perceive that this was what you were meant to think?
Do you not know that I am your end?"

Yeqon was silent in his rage, being mocked by the dying thing.
He dug his thumbs in deeper, tasting the shadow of gray matter
enjoying the spasms of the fleshy parts of the twilight thing.

War of Dictates

"As you fight me blinded to the plight they see, your
     general Lee
walks the white path, wearing a white rag waving the
     white flag.
Your war ends and your plot dies. You live now under
     free skies."

Realizing the subterfuge of a dishonest fight Yeqon
     roared
like the sound of cannon balls in flight, bursting ear
     drums
killing the dying as the wounded struggled beneath
     the titans.
He wrenched his hands apart, pulling at the skull
     until it split
sending bone shrapnel down on a war already lost,
murdering men in their tents and wagons—
and so died Bel, the last of the dragons.

Bunker

(Berlin 4-30-1945)

Azazel stalked the bunker—
the enemy, ancient beyond words had struck a nerve.
In Italy, Gadreel had infected the royalty
had whispered sibilant words of superiority
together they had spread a war of inferiority
cleansing the petty without guilt or pity.
They had accomplished so much, turning war and
    murder
into a machine of industry, new weapons, and new
    methods;
new violent philosophies geared towards the art
of genocide and wiping clean the slate;
of any remnant of the children who killed his.
His son had stalked the earth igniting the planet
with each footfall that fell on fallow fields
hollowing out the lives of weak-willed chattel
cooking their human flesh like cattle on the flames
of steel toothed giants' laughter.
What days those would have been.
To watch his get feast on Enoch's people.
To march alongside the Nephilim
and put violence on a pedestal of holy hymns.

War of Dictates

At first the human sins culminated in wins—
countries fell to the fury of the Fuhrer who went
    further
in capacity for cold calculated violence against
those who would not capitulate in silence.
The air was choked from fires stoked
to rid the land of even the remnants of those revoked.
Azazel evoked the seed of superiority they had planted
so long ago in the Garden outside of Eden.
But even still the ancient grain of hate grew stronger
with every generation it was tilled and sowed and
    grown
until the world choked to deaths strangled on thick
    vines
of egotistical, geographical, and theological folly.
Azazel led this war with purpose
pressing the dangerous into service
slaughtering the surplus of worthless servants.
For so long through history he had spread misery
caused injury to the psyche of a species
bitterly scarred deep even before he had artillery.
But victory was slippery and auxiliary forces
worried at the periphery bitterly taking liberty
contradictory to all Azazel had worked for.

Now news from the south Gadreel's host had been
    lost,
his human vessel tossed onto a stage and left to hang.
Dangled in the wind alongside his closest victims,
a sham left bereft of dignity for his divinity.
But it spoke of the proximity of Sheydim,
the wily king had enlisted Azazel's gifted kindred,
Angels who never fell and who had survived

the first war so many centuries past.
As skilled in the subterfuge of twisting views.
Acting as a muse for propaganda and news.
Hardening the hearts of men to Grigori causes.
It had been the main cause of their losses.
And if he was honest, he needed to be cautious.
This war had turned, and now allies and siblings
were falling, dying, and missing.
Who knew what Isoroku was thinking?
Too few humans held true to the long view
when not under direct control.
When they dragged the new world into the world war
they endangered all they had worked for.
Each step was planned and executed thoughtfully
using strategy that had minds old as humanity.
Now it all turned to dust.

Azazel stepped through the door
and was pleased to see submissive Eva—
so like Eve with her demeanor to please.
He approached her ready to use her,
blow off some steam in the best way possible.
When he realized the darkness was no natural
They were not alone, but his instincts were masterful.
He turned and lifted his gun in one smooth motion.
There in the darkness and silence the notion of eyes.
He fired; the commotion unheard outside the room.
The bullet plucked from the air by a six fingered hand.
Ashmandai again, had broken in and stolen the sound.
Tiresome little slug of a shadow of a man with no
vision.
As Ashmandai melted from shadows, he revealed
others.

War of Dictates

Azazel's brothers, a silent choir of higher fliers.
Winged angels such as Kamdiel who spurned
    compliance
and there was Dumah, which explained the silence.
These were titans who tighten the hold on Azazel's
    games.
Who had joined with the shifting Sheyd to rain on his
    parade
through vengeful actions stifled Semyaza's rightful reign.

Azazel was no weak daft coward as Bazaliel—
he cared more for action and violence
over style or guile unlike the vile Kakobiel.
He would not surrender quietly while his brothers
took him to the place of quiet sunless reflection.
He launched himself towards the six-fingered tart.
Ready to rend and end the offending sprite.
The angel was brought to painful and shameful stop.
The hateful momentum brought up short.
The gun clattered on concrete across the floor.

A hand around Azazel's throat lifted him,
slammed him crushed him into the concrete wall—
spider web of cracks crumbling out from the impact.
Braun held him pinned like a spasming pest where
    twitched
death throws only drove the pin deeper.
The pale skinned blond melted away,
her features, less Aryan, bubbling up
from beneath the primordial ooze of earth
revealing the Semitic glare of dark eyes
set deep in the glowering growling visage of the first
    woman.

John Baltisberger

The proper German clothes dissolved to glorious
    nudity,
a statuesque visage of fertile feminine power.
Curves that were heavy with power and knotted with
    strength.
She was no longer Braun the drawn meek faun,
that illusion withdrawn to one of vengeful female
    brawn.
Lilith's strength was that of all women, the hatred of
    the used
the hurt of the abused who had taken all the pain and
    control
that the phallus-led pompous fools could muster,
and internalized it into a kind of omnipotent power
that could hold back all the fragile masculinity within
    the angel.

"You've met my wife, yes?
Lilith ascended to earth,
she wants words with you.

Well not words really,
she would have violence with you,
an end to your words."

Ashmandai approached then, before the angels.
Before a jury of fury and purely judgmental beings.
He dropped the bullet that the fallen had fired
free from fear as the Grigori was held in a grip
with the power of a species worth of birth pains.
The grip breathed and pushed and squeezed
allowing for no breath or escape for the prone
    watcher.

War of Dictates

"You think we can't kill.
That our dance will continue.
We are doomed to this.

But I wrote the book
Solomon studied so long,
I know all the wards."

From within his cloak of shadow he lifted a bullet,
engraved with the names of things that were
  considered
by some to be gods lifted from the fog of forgotten
  mythologies.
Lines written in languages that even angels lost track
  of
engraved in sanctified steel infused with monstrous
  will.
An intention to murder and trap and contain suffused
  the thing.
He took his time, picking up the pistol that had fallen
as Lilith's grip had tightened and loaded the single
  bullet.
Hourglass pupil eyes studied the gun, Azazel's last gift
  to humanity

"This, your legacy.
Only you should share
in the vast rewards."

Ashmandai pressed the pistol into his hand—
Lilith closed her hand over his,
her fingers crushing the angel's own into the metal.

John Baltisberger

She lifted his hand to his temple.
Azazel fought each moment, muscles tearing
and bones splintering with the effort of struggle.
Every second resisting the titanic strength of the first
    woman.
was a second that his body was ripped apart by his
    own failure.

"Understand angel,
you fight the inevitable.
You have lost the war.

You are weaker now.
Because we have broken you;
your hold on humans.

They have begun to
lose their lust for violence.
They see each other

as human beings;
as fellow living people—
no longer as things.

While you fought this war
trying to kill the bodies,
we fought for their souls.

You will fight no more.
Your freedom, a memory . . .
Winter comes for you."

War of Dictates

Lilith pulled the trigger.
The bullet tore through the Fuhrer
traveling further through the room trailing the gore
of a sloppy gray soup sprinkled with shards of skull
that glistened in the blinking lights of the bunker.
The screams of rage were silent to human ears.
Echoing from the body of the bullet,
a soul shackled in a steel sleeve by strong belief.
Incapable of escaping this new prison Azazel.
The Austrian's body slid to the floor, no longer
    sustained
by the bloody Watcher who had watched as a nation
worked to wipe out a people.
Ashmandai lifted the bullet casing from the floor,
turning it over in hands that had tasted the war.
He would feed the metal to a goat and drive it into the
    wilderness
atoning for the sins of Enoch, allowing them to live

Deplorable

(United States 6-1-2020)

Outside the crowd roared, an entire country up in
    arms
over something that had happened since before the
    country began.
Semyaza had never suspected technology would work
    against him.
He and his had given it to humans, corrupting purity
    with stimulus.
And in the hands of monkeys it became a tool of
    communication.
They shared everything.
Everything.
Every.
Thing.
And at first, he had roared with laughter!
What egotistical little animals, that thought any
    should care about them.
But then.
But.
Then.
Entire coups organized on a platform for sharing
    pictures of food.

War of Dictates

That toppled watcher regime's in countries that
should never fight for freedom.
Semyaza had worn the same suit for decades now,
grown to power
using the technology against them, allowing
corruption to flourish,
it hardly took any effort of will, all it took was a crisp
bill.
Human greed did the rest, he could attest he had put
it to test
again and again; he could get away with anything,
First because of money, and then because of fame.
Avoiding blame with no shame had become a game
played out with people's lives and innocence as both
pieces and prizes.

He could not keep his nature from bloating his form,
from the discoloration from the norm.
But with enough money anything was possible,
not just cash or ass but the promise of more
humans were as hungry as Grigori for more
a never empty pit ready to swallow whole the planet
if it meant just one more dollar for pleasure in their
pocket.
He had spent so many eons alone that now he
surrounded himself
with sycophants and servants and nubile young
things to which he could cling.
Even now, lost in his thoughts he was not alone,
there was a man in the office with him, staring at the
face in the painting
of a man whose smile was made from the teeth of
thrown away slaves.

John Baltisberger

"Listen, I should replace that with a Lincoln.
He was a man of vision, a true Republican."

The words were meaningless to him,
things he spouted that appeased
the least of the beasts and priests that suckled at his power.
That the man did not immediately turn and shower
    him with praise
made him want to scour the man's flesh, toss him
    from a tower
and crush his bones to powder
as once he had done so long ago.

"History will not
remember you as kindly
as it has for either of them."

Though it had been centuries since the reveries
since the memories of his voice had stirred Semyaza,
He could not help but recognize the cadence of his
    acquaintance.
but he had no patience for the craven mewling of
    lesser beings.

"I had wondered when you would come,
half-born king, you shadow thing, you vomited spittle
    lying cur.
You come alone? Where are my brothers? Where are
    my sisters?
Where is your whore-wife, where are the heavy
    hitters?
Where?"

War of Dictates

"All of you delight
in calling my wife a whore.
As though, in insult.

You try so hard to
weaponize her sexuality
but you don't realize.

As I do not own
her body, mind, or her soul
I am not slighted.

You wish you could own
her intense sexuality—
that is why you rage."

Ashmandai shrugged, and as he did
shadow figures peeled off,
copies of the king that spread wing and enclosed the
    beings
in this room together and alone.

"Pretty words, from a pretty bird,
but your tricks are nothing to me.
Kakobiel spreads the word to our herd of stirred
    soldiers.
Bezaliel sings his song to the world, and in no place is
    it louder
than here in my throne room, where ignorance
    trumps science
and power is bliss," the sun kiss Watcher hissed.

John Baltisberger

With a wave of his hand he summoned a table,
out of the pure stuff of creation that he was of.
"I will win this game because human nature is what I
chose.
It is innate in them to hate, for them it is a great faith.
The ate from the apple I offered, not yours, check
mate."

With a splatter and thud the cut head of soulless
Yeqon hit the board
and poured blood spattering the the room with
hissing angel fluids.

"You will lose because
you play a game with humans
while we fight a war.

Gathered outside, look,
they chant for new decency;
they chant against you."

Across the nation and time, the Sheydim had warred,
here they marched to Selma, and there they
demanded blood.
Here a fallen martyr, and there the triumphant war won.
Therefore, he was weakened now, Semyaza realized.
With all his watchers and Grigori in position,
feeding off despair and the poison of dispassionate
disparity.
They had not watched the war as it should be fought
but waited for the Sheyd to make the first move.
And in shadows had they had done so, not out in the
open

but through guile and any opening they flitted like
    flies
breaking apart Watcher lies until all that remained
    was hope.

Semyaza joined Ashmandai at the window,
a proud crowd had gathered shouting hashtag slogans
with enough force to split an ocean and cross into a
    new era of freedom.
They were escaping from bondage at the behest of a
    plague of shadows.
But he would not go quietly into that darkened prison
    once again.
He would break the backs and wills of these would be
    saviors.
Semyaza could feel the bigots rising to the bait,
slathering and crawling over themselves
to ingratiate their bodies for Grigori use.

Ashmandai too knew that it was far from over.
He too was too aware of the flair for the ignorant to
    overpower reason.
for every Watcher in power, firing tear gas into
    crowds
his Sheyd would be on hand in shrouds to dispel
    doubts.
They would offer a drought to Angels who fed on
    spiritual infections.
The vaccine to tyranny was an injection of equity
and humanity was finally ready for the reception and
    retention of freedom.

John Baltisberger

In a blink Ashmandai was gone, he had delivered his
    message
And now the king in orange could sit on his throne
listening to the humming of drumming thrumming
through the open air as cunning humans were
    succumbing to reason
Semyaza knew there was no hiding or running,
despite the centuries of power, the end was coming

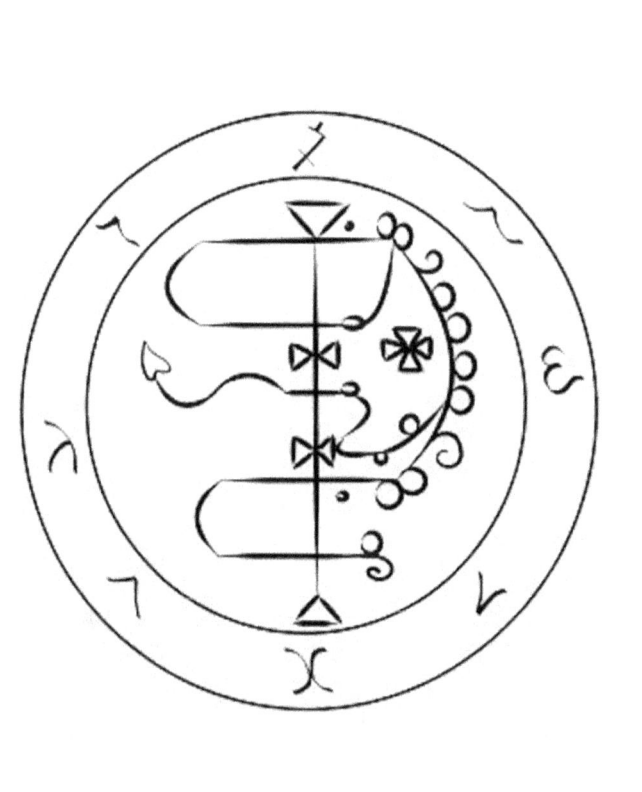

About the Author

John never thought he would write horror or darker fiction, he was planning on writing fantasy. But something about setting all of the occult and fantastical elements of fantasy just behind the backdrop of the modern world appealed to him, and he wanted to introduce the world to the incredible mythology of mythic Judaism. He spends his time squirreled away fervently working on the next book or engaging in the 'Obliterate the Globe' project, only taking breaks to record episodes of Madness Heart Radio and Wandering Monster, or to eat, or to play with puppies. John lives with his patient and gorgeous wife Desiree, and maniacal and powerful daughter Aziza. You can find him and the project at www.KaijuPoet.com